"Henry Flesh, a cartographer of unkind worlds, sends in his writing a ferocious and also forgiving dispatch: Consciousness costs. Like a frightening early-morning dream, his prose takes his characters and his readers right up to the vertiginous edge of consciousness, daring us to wake up, to open our eyes, to see what we now see. His debut novel, *Massage*, introduced an unflinching voice, an unsparing eye, an uncompromising moral vision, an unnerving acknowledgment of the injuries we inflict on each other. He resists sentimentality, but he does not resist the humanity that flickers and dwells within his characters—the hustlers, the celestial spirits (or those who are both), and much more, all at once—as they hang on to unkind worlds using little more than their fingernails. *Michael*, a work stamped with Flesh's febrile narrative touch, is a novel of explosions. Singular lives explode, as do worlds, as does, most importantly, one kind of human consciousness itself."   —Ellen Miller, author of *Like Being Killed*

"Funny, tightly plotted, and just two shades darker than burnt coffee. Henry Flesh has crafted a fine and disturbing novel."   —David Sedaris, author of *Me Talk Pretty One Day* and *Naked, on Massage*

"Henry Flesh must be lauded for his courage as well as his talent."   —Kaylie Jones, author of *Celeste Ascending* and *A Soldier's Daughter Never Cries*

MICHAEL

Henry Flesh

With illustrations by

John H. Greer

Akashic Books
New York

This is a work of fiction. All names, characters, places, and incidents are the product of the author's imagination. Any resemblance to real events or persons, living or dead, is entirely coincidental.

Published by Akashic Books
©2000 Henry Flesh
Illustrations © 2000 John H. Greer

Illustrations by John H. Greer
Design and layout by Fritz Michaud for Generation Squirrel
Author photo by Nina Subin

ISBN: 1-888451-12-2
Library of Congress Catalog Card Number: 00-101837

Akashic Books
PO Box 1456
New York, NY 10009
email: Akashic7@aol.com
website: www.akashicbooks.com

To my friend Nathan,
who embodies for me
the light in this book

ACKNOWLEDGMENTS

I would like to express my gratitude once again to Johnny Temple at Akashic Books for his extraordinary dedication, support, and generosity; to Fritz Michaud, the book's designer; and to Kara Gilmour and Johanna Ingalls for their editorial assistance. I would like to thank, too, John H. Greer for his remarkable illustrations; and Ellen Adamson, O.B. Crowder, Joseph Cummins, Gabrielle Danchick, and Mark Sullivan for their invaluable editorial input.

Also, for their help and encouragement, I would like to thank Paul Calderon, Kate Christensen, James Hoff, Kaylie Jones, Wendy Lochner, Tim McLoughlin, Lena Ross, Thaddeus Rutkowski, Janyce Stefan-Cole, Nina Subin, Liz Szabla, and John Wynne.

PART I
THE CHILDREN OF
MICHAEL

The car revving up outside sounded for an instant like a gun going off, but Stephen hardly noticed the noise. He lay still, curled up on his bed in the hot, lifeless air, trying to forget what he'd recalled on awakening at nine, an hour earlier: This was the anniversary he'd been dreading, July 15. Robert died three years ago today.

"Motherfucker!" someone screamed on the street, and he gripped the sheets, staring at the television set in front of him, wondering if he should switch it on. Church bells pealed outside, and he realized it was Sunday. There'd probably be a lot of news shows on now. Pundits would be talking about the recent spate of suspected terrorist activities, the unexplained downings of more than a dozen commercial airplanes, or maybe discussing the deepening crisis in Russia, that seemingly endless revolt in Chechnya and a new, bloody border dispute with Ukraine. Hell, he thought, let it all blow to bits. Everything was fucked.

He contemplated getting up, maybe going out for breakfast. But he couldn't really afford to go anywhere; his unemployment check, the second to last owed him from his most recent proofreading job, wouldn't come for another five or six days. He knew what he'd find outside anyway, the detritus of a Saturday night on New York's Lower East Side. He could just imagine the garbage spilling from the trash bin at the corner, practically knew which of the neighborhood junkies would be passed out on his doorway. Nothing would surprise him.

He heard the sound of a siren—coming from a police car, he assumed—then a helicopter flying over his building. He suspected that the helicopter belonged to the police as well, that some crime had occurred in the vicinity, a robbery or a murder. An unpleasant heaviness swept over him. He wanted his surroundings to seem soothing. He wanted to feel safe.

Rolling over, he touched his balding head and sighed. I'm getting old, he thought; forty-nine's over the hill.

Just then, as the sound of the helicopter faded, his buzzer rang. He hesitated for a second, then lumbered out of bed, slowly, conscious of his protruding stomach and fat thighs. He tossed on his clothes and walked to the speaker. *"What?"* he screamed into it, surprised by his fury. "Who's there?"

"It's the Children of Michael," a man's voice answered. "We have good news for you, brother."

Shit, Stephen said to himself, those fucking ghouls. He glanced behind him at his apartment, which was extremely neat but appeared barren. Everything was arranged as it had been during his eleven years with Robert, his bed in the same corner, a chest of drawers directly across from it, a shabby blue rug on the floor. He'd never been able to change a thing; it all reminded him so much of his old life. He turned back to the speaker and stared at it, then took a long breath. What the fuck? he thought. What else was he going to do? Moving quickly, he pressed the buzzer.

Stephen had heard a great deal about the Children of Michael in the past few months and had seen representatives of that cult on nearly every street corner, passing out pamphlets and flyers, announcing what they claimed was the impending end of the world. He paid no attention to them, just as he'd ignored every other cult he'd seen over the years, all the ones that had cropped up since the sixties, the Hare Krishnas and Aesthetic Realists, Jesus Freaks, Moonies, and Scientologists, countless others. It seemed to him that the Children of Michael were more widespread and omnipresent than these earlier groups had been, although, he considered, he might have gotten that impression from the fact that this cult had appeared for the first time only recently and had

immediately eclipsed every other. It was as if the Children of Michael were everywhere at the moment.

He was exhausted, not having slept well, and his vision was cloudy—the air in the hallway outside his apartment thickly humid, appearing misty through his fatigue, watery and dreamlike—so it was jarring for him to see three of them climbing the stairs and coming toward him as he stood inside by the apartment's open door: a pale, twentyish white man in jeans and a lightweight blue shirt, very good-looking, he noticed; a heavyset black woman, thirty-nine or forty, wearing a loose, dark dress; and a young black girl, a child around ten. He realized he'd seen the girl in his neighborhood, both during the day and at night, always on her own. Each time he'd seen her, he'd found her eerie, preternaturally reflective and subdued for her age, not at all like the other children he saw on his block, most of whom appeared to run in packs, smoking cigarettes and selling joints, stealing candy from the local stores. This girl, prim and plain-looking in her faded green dress, seemed to exist in a world of her own. Despite her strangeness, he found her huge brown eyes extraordinarily intelligent, calm, and hypnotic. He stepped out into the hallway.

"Good morning, brother," the young man greeted him. His voice was deep and pleasant.

Stephen thought that he sounded sexy and stared at his face, then at the black hair falling across his brow, finally at his lanky frame. There was something about him, he wasn't sure what—maybe his clear skin, the thickness of his hair, or his build, maybe just his youth—something that reminded him of Robert. He lowered his eyes. What difference does it make? he asked himself. Robert's dead.

"Have you heard the good news?" the young man continued, his tone bright, his manner easy. "The end is near."

"Look, I'm busy," Stephen muttered, turning away from him, suddenly impatient, regretting that he had buzzed them in. He couldn't imagine what had come over him; he'd acted without thinking.

"Timothy here, he's a preacher," the heavyset woman chimed in, gesturing toward the young man, an almost palpable joy in her voice and eyes. "He knows: The end *is* near. We don't have long. It could come at any time." Smiling, she exclaimed, "Oh, Lord, I hope it comes soon. Today would be a beautiful day to meet Jesus."

Timothy grinned at her. "Right, Ruth," he said cheerfully. "Amen, praise the Lord, and thank you, Michael."

Stephen again noted how handsome Timothy was, beautiful really, his dark hair providing a wonderful contrast to his pale skin and blue eyes. He sensed a tug inside himself, a longing. He thought of all the young men who'd be outside at the moment, some stumbling home from clubs, exactly like he used to do, others just awakening, out to buy the Sunday papers. He thought of men he'd known in the past, friends and lovers, like Victor, Jesse, Paul, all the others who'd died. He thought of Robert.

"Have you been saved yet?" Ruth asked him, her soft, round face erupting into another smile. "Do you know Michael?"

Stephen looked from Timothy to her, thinking—unexpectedly, for the first time in years—of Ethel, the cook his parents had employed when he was a child in Indiana. He remembered sitting in the kitchen when his parents were away, watching as Ethel prepared his meal, singing gospel songs as she worked or, in that kind, unruffled voice of hers, telling him stories she'd heard at the ramshackle old Pentecostal church she attended in their small town, stories of Jesus and the prophets, of a Judgment Day that had been foretold in the Bible, in the Book of Revelation. The details of these stories were vague to Stephen after all these years. He only recalled Ethel's saying that God's judgments would be immediate when they happened, severe yet just, that those deemed sinners would be thrown down into the fires of Hades, and that the believers, God's children, would join Him in Heaven for an eternity of bliss. As Stephen grew older, Ethel's stories began to seem preposterous to him. In spite of this, the kindness she continued to display toward him whenever they were together affected him deeply. Remembering Ethel now, as he stood in the heat of his building's murky hallway, he fixed his eyes more closely on Ruth's smiling face and sensed traces of that old affection spilling through him, with the humid air.

Ruth touched the arm of the young girl beside her. "My baby Charlene has something for you," she told Stephen gently.

Stephen flushed, embarrassed by the emotions his memories had stirred in him.

Charlene raised a hand, her eyes grave, and held up a small navy-blue pamphlet, the picture on its cover one of clouds floating across a dark, threatening sky.

Stephen took the pamphlet from her and read the title, "Rejoice in the Night to Come," allowing its thin paper to rest against the moistening palm of his right hand.

"We must be ready," Timothy declared fervently, his face glowing. He looked, Stephen felt, almost adolescent, like Robert at eighteen, the age Robert had been when Stephen had met him—passionate, too, like Robert in bed.

Raising his voice, Timothy went on: "The Bible says, 'For the Lord Himself shall descend from Heaven with a shout, with the voice of an archangel, and with the trump of God.' That time shall be with us very soon."

Unnerved by Timothy's zealous tone, by its curious contrast to his guileless appearance, Stephen slipped back toward his apartment's doorway. He stopped, his eyes returning to Timothy's face, which now seemed extraordinarily placid. He didn't want to be alone, he realized, alone and thinking about Robert.

Charlene inched past Stephen, through his apartment's open door and into his kitchen. Once inside, she glanced around—at the clean dishes placed neatly in the rack by the sink, at a print of an Impressionist painting on the wall, and at a large oak table. She walked up to the table and ran her fingers across its surface, then headed toward an open window at the back of the room.

"Now what's that girl doing?" Ruth shook her head, then looked at Stephen. "Don't pay Charlene no mind, mister. You can't say nothing to her. She's deaf as a stone."

Despite his growing apprehension, Stephen was fascinated by everything he was seeing and feeling. All of it felt unreal: Charlene's strange behavior; the humidity in the air; his desire for Timothy—his *hunger* for him, for what he made him remember, what he seemed to represent. Dazed, he watched Charlene make her way to the window, then stand still, peering onto the alleyway outside. Another helicopter passed over his building.

"Oh, yes, my baby's deaf," Ruth murmured, nodding. "Born that way, you understand. Mute, too. It don't matter none, though, thank you, Michael. And praise Jesus." She grinned. "Charlene, she got the Voice."

"The Voice?" Stephen kept his eyes on Charlene's back, conscious of the heat, which was even more miserable than it had been the day before, listening as the noise of the helicopter dimmed. "What do you mean?"

"Charlene's Michael's prophet," Timothy answered, then, reverently, lowering his voice: "Michael speaks God's word through her. Ruth's the interpreter. She's the only one who can tell us what Michael says to Charlene."

"Oh, yeah?" Stephen looked from Charlene to Ruth, then at Timothy, who smiled at him—very openly, it seemed. For a second Stephen was sure that he caught something flirta-

tious in his eyes. He placed a hand on his own right thigh, felt how fleshy it was, and immediately pulled his hand away.

Charlene turned from the window and gazed at Stephen, raising one hand with urgency, beckoning him to come inside the apartment to her.

Stephen saw a faint, hazy white light around her head. It disappeared, and he shivered. I'm just tired, he thought. Uneasy, he tried to laugh, but couldn't. He turned to Ruth and Timothy and forced himself to smile. "I think she's trying to tell us something, don't you?"

Their eyes on Charlene, neither replied. Both appeared attentive, then concerned.

Stephen felt more peculiar than ever. Nothing made sense to him; he just knew that he didn't want to be alone. Hesitant, again speaking to Ruth and Timothy, he mumbled, "Why don't you two come in for a while? I could make us some coffee."

Not hearing this, Ruth hurried past him, rushing through the doorway, then to the window, to Charlene. "What is it, baby?" she asked her breathlessly.

Stephen pivoted toward them, stepping inside. Timothy followed him.

Light again encircled Charlene's head, much brighter this time. She was shaking, her eyes wide open, her mouth as well, and she appeared to be forming silent words. Ruth grabbed her arms and held onto her tightly. Overwhelmed, Stephen shut his eyes.

"There, there, baby, come on, what is it?" Ruth whispered to Charlene. "What did Michael tell you? Is it coming? Are we gonna meet Jesus?"

Stephen opened his eyes. The light around Charlene was gone, and she was no longer shaking, but was staring at him.

"What is it, honey, what's going on?" Ruth asked her. "Tell your mama what Michael's been saying to you." She placed a hand under Charlene's chin, tilted her head up, and gazed into her eyes, then nodded. "Uh-huh. Yes. Yes, baby." Smiling, she looked at Stephen and spoke rapidly: "My baby here, she had a vision. You was in it."

Stephen flinched, moving back.

Ruth's grin grew broader, and she nearly laughed. "Michael's coming," she said, thrilled. "You're gonna meet him. Charlene says it's gonna happen soon."

"What is?" Stephen felt surges of heat passing through him. "Who…?" He hurried to a chair near the oak table and sat down, took a deep breath, and tried to speak. "I mean, what…who's Michael?" was all he could say.

Ruth and Timothy looked at him with amazement. An expression of distinct pity crossed their faces. Charlene moved from the window and came to his side, taking hold of his right hand. Her skin felt smooth to Stephen, soothingly warm, and her eyes looked serene and imperturbable. It seemed to him that he could sink into them if he wanted to, become enveloped by her. He felt profoundly sad.

Timothy and Ruth moved to his side as well.

"Michael is one of the Lord's archangels," Timothy explained to Stephen, his voice boyish despite its deep pitch— so sexy, Stephen thought. "He's God's favorite one. He visited the prophet Daniel in prison, and he'll be here on Judgment Day, along with the Angel Gabriel, after the Days of Rapture."

Timothy's words seemed to shoot through Stephen to his core. Years ago Ethel had told him what Timothy was telling him. Timothy's voice began to sound oddly authoritative, as if no longer his own. Stephen couldn't understand what he said, and he could barely keep his eyes open. He wondered if this was a dream, if he'd drifted off hours before.

"When Michael speaks to Charlene, he speaks for God and for Jesus, with a voice that blares like a trumpet but is meek as a lamb's," Ruth trilled, her face joyous, again reminding Stephen of those nights when Ethel used to take care of him, of all the times that his parents were away. "He's like Gabriel, only greater than him, greater than all the other angels in Heaven."

Stephen tried to grasp what Ruth was saying, though he wasn't certain why he was so desperate to understand her, why he felt so strange and so moved. Charlene squeezed his hand, and he squeezed hers. He realized there were tears on his cheeks.

"Oh, child," Ruth whispered to him. Charlene squeezed his hand again.

Stephen looked from Ruth to Timothy, then, indistinctly, thought that he saw Robert as he'd been one evening years before, at a Talking Heads concert in Central Park, smiling sweetly while sipping a glass of wine. They'd gone to the concert with friends of theirs, a couple named Jesse and Paul, both long since dead, and the four of them had shared a picnic on a hill near the concert stage. "Robert?" Stephen said now, speaking in Timothy's direction. Robert's image faded.

Timothy said something, but Stephen couldn't understand him. "What's that?" he asked.

Timothy spoke once more. Though his words sounded muffled, Stephen was sure that he heard him say, "He that cometh after me is mightier than I, whose shoes I am not worthy to bear."

Ruth and Charlene moved closer to Timothy, Charlene still holding Stephen's hand.

Stephen felt Charlene's soft skin. "What did you say?" he asked Timothy.

Timothy gazed at him, then spoke with a marked sympathy, his words now completely audible, his tone tender: "I was just wondering if you were okay."

Stephen raised a hand to his face and touched his tears. Embarrassed by them, he wanted to lie and say he was fine, ask everyone to leave, go back to bed, and try to sleep again. Yet the warmth he saw in Timothy's eyes seemed to be pulling something out of him. "No. No, I'm not," he replied quickly. He blushed. He didn't know why he'd admitted this, why he'd spoken at all.

Timothy, Ruth, and Charlene kept their eyes on him, studying him with obvious affection. No one budged. Then

Charlene stroked his hand, and Timothy produced a dim smile, whispering, "Go on."

Stephen felt as if he had no choice, that he had to speak. Words gushed out: "It's just that…it's just that I hate my life, I hate myself. I feel as if everything's over, that it ended a long time ago. I'm broke, I haven't worked since this fucking recession started. And I…I'm lonely. It's like…Christ, almost all my friends are dead! I mean, there's this woman Sharon, but she lost her job like me, so she's Upstate, with her parents for the summer. And then there's Peter, he was my best friend, but he's really sick now, demented. My family doesn't give a shit about me, they never have. I'm broke, I may be sick myself, I may be dying, but I don't want to be tested, I can't be, I don't want to find out. It's all…" He drew in his breath, sobbing.

Timothy touched Stephen's arm. "Yes?" he asked softly. "Just let it out. Come on, you can do it."

Stephen looked up. Timothy's face appeared incredibly kind.

"Please," Timothy went on. "Trust us. Trust Michael."

Stephen felt Timothy's hand caressing him. "It's…it's my…" He shuddered, then took a deep breath. "It's my lover, it's Robert. He's dead, too."

Timothy continued stroking Stephen's arm. "Yes," he said. "We know."

Stephen stopped crying. "Wh…what?"

"He's with God, like so many others. But he'll only be away for a little while longer."

Stephen gazed into Timothy's clear blue eyes, awed, then disturbed, not comprehending. He'd spoken without thinking when he'd mentioned Robert, yet Timothy—and, apparently, these other two—seemed to know about him, who he was, maybe more. This *is* a dream, he told himself; it *has* to be.

Timothy smiled. "Michael's coming, Michael and God. Robert'll be with them."

"Oh, yes!" Ruth said.

Charlene threw her arms over Stephen's shoulders and placed her head on his chest. She had a fresh, powdery scent. Stephen wanted to return her embrace, but couldn't. Somehow that seemed impossible.

"It's the End Time," Timothy continued. "War and disease, poverty and hunger, we see it everywhere, more than ever before. But we knew this would happen. God told us that it would many times in the Bible. 'And there shall be signs in the sun,' He said in the Book of Luke, 'and in the moon, and in the stars, and upon the earth, distress of nations…' Well, it's started. And now that it has, people, the blessed, are being called by Michael to God."

"The Rapture!" Ruth cried excitedly, beaming.

"Yes." Timothy's eyes darted to Ruth, then back to Stephen. "But those chosen to be raptured are not only those who've accepted Christ, as we were once taught. Michael has shown us how petty it is to think in this way. God is much more merciful than that." He looked at Stephen empathetically, deliberately and carefully. "No, some are chosen for other reasons, chosen because God has seen that they've suffered enough. Perhaps it's time for you to be raptured, too."

Stephen cringed and looked at the floor. He couldn't believe what was going on.

Ruth closed her eyes, praying: "Oh, Lord, our suffering is almost over! Timothy and I are being called to You soon. That's what Charlene said Michael told her. Yes, that's what she said. Dear Jesus, it's gonna happen. We're being called to You even before my baby Charlene."

Charlene pushed her face against Stephen's chest, breathing quickly, then gasping. Stephen's muscles grew more rigid. He didn't move.

" 'In a moment,' " Timothy quoted passionately, " 'in the twinkling of an eye, the dead shall be changed.' That's from I Corinthians. It's all in the Bible. I Thessalonians says that 'the dead in Christ shall rise first: Then we which are alive and remain shall be caught up together with them in the clouds, to meet the Lord in the air: and so shall we ever be with the Lord.' " He gazed steadily at Stephen, then continued, eager: "Thousands have been raptured already, many when they were sick, Robert and all the others. It wasn't really AIDS that took most of them, like the doctors said. Oh, no! Strange things have happened to other people as well. Look at the ones who've disappeared in the sky, in those exploding planes. Everyone thinks these were terrorist acts. Believe me, that's not so. No, the people who disappeared in this way and those taken by AIDS, they were chosen by God, chosen to come to Him because of their suffering in this life. We Children of Michael want to be chosen, too, raptured during these Years of Tribulation that we're going through, these years of horror we were warned about, the ones that'll only end when God comes down from Heaven, comes down with His angels, with those who've died and those who've been raptured, comes down to judge both the living and the dead, to establish His kingdom on Earth. That's what Michael's been trying to tell us. That's why he's coming here, to save us, just as Jesus did before."

Stephen noticed Charlene staring at him. The light was around her head, becoming brighter, until it seemed as if he were spinning into it. He felt faint.

Timothy leaned forward, placing an arm across Stephen's shoulder. "Is everything all right?" he asked, his voice very low. "Are you sleepy?"

Stephen looked back at Timothy, nodding weakly, completely enervated.

"Well, you can sleep if you want to. It's safe. Michael'll be here soon. God's kingdom is coming."

Stephen shut his eyes. He felt Timothy reach under his arms, pull him up from his chair, and lead him toward the bedroom. In the distance, outside, he heard another helicopter. He tried to open his eyes, but found it too difficult.

"Just relax," Timothy whispered as they approached the bed. "You can relax now." He pulled Stephen's shirt over his head and unclasped his pants.

Stephen quivered. He could feel Timothy's hands on his thighs, undressing him, his fingers grazing his penis, just briefly. When he was naked, he was surprised that he wasn't embarrassed, humiliated that Timothy could see his body. He opened his eyes and glanced toward the kitchen. Ruth was on her knees, praying, Charlene standing beside her. Then, as Stephen watched, Charlene rose a few feet above the floor into the air.

Timothy kissed Stephen's neck. Stephen looked into his eyes.

"You've nothing to be ashamed of, you know," Timothy said. "The Children of Michael isn't about shame, and it's not about guilt. Those others, all those preachers and evangelists who came before us, they were wrong." He moved his mouth to Stephen's and kissed his lips, then pulled back. "The last thing we need now is to feel guilty, particularly about love." Smiling, he stroked Stephen's arms. "No, we can never feel guilty about that. Not anymore."

Stephen wavered, gazing at Timothy, whose eyes appeared remarkably gentle. Moving abruptly, in one desperate motion, he pulled himself closer to him, pressed his body against his, and held him tightly. The noise of the helicopter outside was overpowering and was joined by the sound of police sirens. He peered over Timothy's shoulder and saw Charlene floating across the kitchen, the white light now surrounding her entire body. Ruth was still on her knees, praying intently and looking, in ways he couldn't quite understand, much more like Ethel.

"We've had enough shame," Timothy went on. He slid the fingers of his right hand across Stephen's chest. "Enough guilt. We have to learn to love one another, find out once more how to do it. Michael and God are coming. We have to be ready for them." He moved his hand around to Stephen's back and stroked his shoulders.

Stephen pressed his body further into Timothy's and at that moment sensed, somehow knew, that he wasn't overweight any longer. His stomach was flat, his muscles taut, his hairline

not receding. He was trim and fit, like men he'd seen outside, men he'd desired. Years seemed to have been lifted from him. The sound of the helicopter and police sirens grew louder. Far

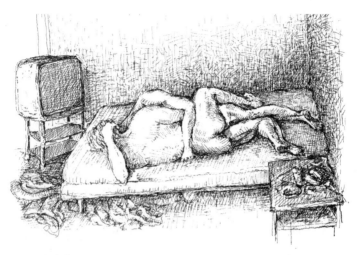

away, behind Timothy, in the kitchen, Charlene was floating toward the open window.

"Let's lie down," Timothy murmured, pulling Stephen nearer to the bed. "Just you and me."

Timothy undressed, revealing a body as tight and smooth as Stephen's own had become. They lay on the sheets, closely entwined. Beneath the roar of the helicopter and the wail of police sirens, Stephen heard Ruth praying: "Michael, come to us. Deliver us from everything. Charlene's going to you now. She's gonna find out if God's ready for Timothy and me, then come back and let us know. But please, Michael, let Him be ready. *Please!*" Stephen looked up, into the next room. Charlene was gliding out the window, her green dress no longer faded, instead luminescent and jewel-like. Timothy caressed Stephen's shoulders and thighs. Stephen caressed his in return. He shut his eyes and was soon asleep.

2

Stephen awoke, distraught to find himself alone. Late-afternoon sunlight shot into his eyes, and he shook his head, then noticed the rolls of his gut. He sighed. Nothing seemed to have changed; apparently he *had* been dreaming. He seized his pack of Marlboros from the bedside table, lit a cigarette, and curled onto his side. He didn't know what he could do now. He didn't want to do a thing.

As he lay chain-smoking, he found it hard to accept that what he'd had was a dream; his recollection of the morning felt vivid and real. Then, too, he was naked, and he nearly always wore something to bed. He was almost certain he'd done so the night before. Still, what he remembered had been totally improbable, frightening as well—even lying with the nude, handsome boy.

Touching his groin, he stared at a picture hanging on the wall, Robert's portrait of their cat Rose, who'd died shortly after Robert had painted her. Robert had never really been an artist, Stephen knew, just a dabbler. This work, like his others, was pedestrian, gray and unimaginative. Yet its very familiarity assured Stephen that what he recalled from the morning could never have occurred.

He drew another cigarette from his pack and struck a match. As he lit up, he heard a low-flying helicopter whirring outside, just above his building. His pulse began to race. Terrified, he grabbed the phone from the bedside table and started to dial his friend Sharon at her parents' house in Schenectady. He stopped. Sharon had said something when he'd talked to her the day before, he recalled, something that had upset him, though he could no longer remember what it was. Puzzled and disturbed, he took a deep drag on his cigarette.

The sound of the helicopter outside grew dim, and he rose unsteadily from his bed. He found his robe on a nearby chair and put it on, then walked into the living room, to a window that faced the street, and stared out into the bright sunshine. The usual crowd of teenage boys was gathered by the curb, many, he knew, dealing drugs. Two were arguing, glowering at each other, their voices raised. "Come on, man!" one cried. "Get over it!" The radio the second boy carried was playing a popular salsa tune, a song Stephen had heard coming up from the street several times in recent weeks: "I like you, baby. Oooh, baby, I like you a lot." The song's upbeat tempo made him think of music that he'd heard years before, of lazy Sunday afternoons in the summer when he and Robert would stand together by this window smoking joints, looking out onto a street shimmering in the sunshine, just as it was today, at the teenage dealers, at mothers pushing babies in strollers, at the pedestrians hurrying by. As he listened now to the music coming from below—"Yeah, baby, I like you a lot"— he could almost feel Robert's presence beside him.

Just then, with a shock, he recalled what Sharon had said that had upset him. It was a remark she'd made just after he had spoken wistfully of the past, of parties and clubs that he'd gone to with Robert, Sharon, and Peter years ago: "Come on, Stephen, don't dwell on all that shit. You really shouldn't romanticize those things. It wasn't always that great. You of all people should know *that*." As she spoke, Stephen envisioned Robert as he'd been so often, stoned and moody, uncommunicative—exactly the way, Stephen knew, he himself could be. "What do you mean, 'me of all people'?" he screamed into the phone. "What're you trying to say? Is it because Robert and I used to fight? So what? Doesn't everyone?" "Forget it!" Sharon snapped and quickly changed the subject.

He stared at the street. The two boys who'd been arguing were now sharing a joint and laughing. He barely saw them. The fierce sun, slowly sinking in the sky, hit his eyes and nearly blinded him. He felt a sensation that had become familiar, especially at night when he couldn't sleep, a sensation of being trapped within his body, apart from everyone else and absolutely alone. This sensation frightened him, as it always did, and he wanted to fling himself outward beyond the window, to float through the air—like Charlene, he thought—to become one with the boys on the street and with the world out there.

That's completely fantastic, he told himself; I just dreamed about Charlene.

He swirled around, then rushed to the bedroom and crawled back into bed, wanting a joint or a drink. He had a headache and wondered if he'd had too much to drink after he and Sharon had talked, if he'd gotten very drunk. Perhaps he'd passed out at some point. He'd been doing that a lot lately.

He thought about their conversation. Sharon hadn't meant any harm, he decided; she'd only been trying to help him. That was the way she'd always been. Most of the time he was grateful for her advice and solicitude, her kindness. God knows he'd needed it since Robert had died. No one else left could understand him as she did, could be such a good friend. Peter was much too sick, beyond the assistance that any doctor could provide. And he knew that he couldn't expect anything of his parents; he hadn't spoken to either of them in years.

He looked toward the bedside table, suddenly angry, and saw a half-smoked joint in an ashtray. He lit it and took several quick drags. He wanted to squelch the fury he felt and a vague sadness just beneath that. He took a longer drag and absentmindedly switched on the TV, keeping the volume down, paying no attention to the image that came on, feeling the pot take effect. He thought of something else that Sharon had said to him the night before, just prior to her hanging up: "God, Stephen, what's gotten into you lately? You never used to be like this. You've gotten so bitter." He hadn't been able to respond. He'd known at the time—just as he knew this afternoon—that Sharon was right.

He directed his attention toward the TV and saw two newscasters, an older man with white hair and a pert young blonde woman, excitedly discussing whatever had occurred that day. The words "Crisis in Russia" were conspicuous in the background, along with a photograph of Russia's recently elected president, Porfiry Petrovitch, a fat, balding, red-faced man in his early sixties. Petrovitch was a staunch nationalist who lately had been making ominous threats to two of his country's adversaries, Chechnya and Ukraine, hinting at his readiness to use nuclear weapons. Studying his picture, Stephen finished the joint, then mumbled, "Fuck him. Fuck them all." He glanced from Petrovitch to the blonde newscaster, thinking for a second that in her facile brightness, she resembled his mother as she had appeared to him when he was around six.

He sensed the pot eddying through him, then, precipitately, had a crystal-clear vision of his life as a child, remembering how reserved and miserable he'd been. His family had money and were firmly entrenched in the upper-middle class of their Indiana town. They owned a large house at the top of a hill, an estate actually, with many acres, a swimming pool, and tennis courts. Ethel and his parents' other servants had taken care of him; it was apparent even back then that his mother and father weren't interested in him, that he was secondary to their social lives. Both only rarely displayed the parental concern that he'd craved. Among the few happy memories he had of his childhood were those of himself alone in the woods near their house, by a large pond in a clearing.

He continued staring toward the TV, no longer seeing anything, recalling how, after graduating from college, he'd been anxious to cut all ties with his family and so, in a piqued, uncharacteristic outburst one evening, declared to them his homosexuality, newly acknowledged even to himself. This penetrated his parents' indifference and infuriated them. "You're ruining your life!" his mother cried once he'd broken the news. She was preparing to go to a dinner party, finishing a drink as she fussed with the hem of her red, glittering evening dress, then played with a strand of her freshly coiffed blonde hair. His father said nothing, only shook his head in disgust. "God, Stephen," his mother added, angrier, "you're always doing this sort of thing to me."

Stephen bolted out of the house and drove to a bar downtown. The next day he withdrew from his bank the principal of a small inheritance he'd received from his maternal grandmother. Three days later he moved to New York. There, captivated by what he found, doing his best to forget all that he'd known and not think about his mother and father, he felt his anger become dormant once more.

His parents made a few attempts to contact him, halfhearted and perfunctory ones, Stephen thought. He tried to act as impassively as he could whenever they called. Then, six months after he'd left Indiana, he received a letter from his father. Even after all these years he could still remember every word. "It has become obvious to your mother and me," it read, "that you don't appreciate all the advantages we've given you and that you don't intend to live the way we always have. That is unfortunate. Perhaps some day you'll see the error of your ways, though I fear this may never happen. Until such a time as it does, however, and you see fit to apologize to us for your selfish and foolish choices, we think it best that there be no further communication between us. I remain, regretfully, your father." Stephen never spoke to anyone in his family after this.

An old song wafted up from the street, drawing him back, a ballad sung by someone who'd been popular years before, a woman with a deep alto voice: "It was one of those days, but it's far away now. I'm just a lonely girl in her room without her man. He's gone, and he won't return. Things aren't the same. They'll never be that way again."

Stephen couldn't remember when he'd first heard this; he just knew that it had been a long time ago. It affected him despite its sentimentality. The cacophony of music that he heard day and night on the street, coming from the radios of people loitering near his building, often pulled him out of himself, back to other times. "He'll never return, things'll never be the same," the woman sang, and Stephen thought that he was about to cry.

He stared at the picture on the muted TV, forcing himself to focus on it, and saw an airplane in flames on a mountaintop. This image appeared completely unreal and seemed very distant. Another plane's been hit, he conjectured, and felt a grim satisfaction. He wished his parents had been on that plane or on one of the others that had gone down; maybe then he'd inherit some money. But he knew this wouldn't happen, that undoubtedly he would be disinherited. His parents were probably at home in Indiana right now, still sprightly despite the fact that they were in their late seventies, carrying on vapidly, hating him as much as he hated them—that is, if they weren't totally unmindful of his existence.

"Far away," the woman sang from outside, and he thought about Robert. Robert had meant everything to him, it seemed, and yet, recalling once more his conversation with Sharon, he remembered how disillusioned he'd become as Robert had withdrawn into himself, how impatient he'd been with him. The silent, moody Robert he'd started to see wasn't the exuberant, unrestrained boy he'd loved. Most of the joy they'd experienced early on had faded as the years passed. Then Robert got sick. When he died, it appeared to Stephen now, too much—everything—had been left unspoken.

"It was one of those days," the woman went on slowly, repeating the refrain, "and I'm just a lonely girl. A lonely girl in her room."

He realized that he knew this song from the mid-seventies, when he'd moved to New York. Those were amazing days, he thought, not like today, with all the shit that's gone down. He'd taken full advantage of what had been available, the clubs and nightlife, the sexual freedom, the sense of unlimited possibilities, of discovery. It had been incredibly liberating for him after Indiana, those horrid years with his parents. He recalled the men he'd had back then, so many of them, and touched his belly, sure that he'd never be able to have anyone again. Despite this, he was acutely conscious of the fact that he was the same man who had danced all night in after-hours clubs, who'd screwed strangers in parks and sucked them off in the back rooms of seedy bars.

"Just a lonely girl," the woman on the radio continued with a flourish, ending the song. "Yes, a lonely girl without her man."

He shot upright, desperate for a drink. There was a large jug of white wine in the refrigerator, he remembered—at least there would be if he hadn't finished it the night before. He glanced at the TV and saw Porfiry Petrovitch addressing a large assembly, pounding the podium with his fists. Stupid fuck, Stephen thought, and stood. He hurried to the kitchen.

As he'd hoped, the jug of wine was in the refrigerator, though only a third of the bottle was left. He took hold of it, found a tall glass in the dish rack by the sink, and returned to the bedroom with the jug and glass in his hands.

He lay on his bed and, feeling the heat, filled his glass with wine and gulped half of it down. An announcement came on the radio playing outside, the speaker's voice loud and surprisingly shaky. Stephen couldn't tell what he was saying. He looked toward the TV. A video clip of soldiers mobilizing near a mountain pass was being aired. He assumed they were Russians, in Chechnya maybe, or perhaps in Ukraine. He wondered what was happening; there were so many of them, probably thousands. The words "Breaking News" flashed across the screen, and the two newscasters he'd seen before reappeared, speaking, it seemed, even more excitedly than they had earlier. He considered turning up the volume, but felt too high. I don't need to hear any of this shit, he thought. He finished his wine, picked up the jug, and poured more into his glass, then rolled onto his side.

On his bedside table's lower shelf he saw a magazine that he recalled thumbing through the night before, a glossy, softcore pornographic pictorial entitled *Dewy Boys*, full of images of nude Czechoslovakian youths, all taken by a well-known fashion photographer. Stephen had bought the magazine over a year ago. Though many of the photos in it aroused him, he'd been a little amused at first by what he saw as the photographer's pretensions—the overly soft focus used in the images, the self-consciously arty, misty sheen given each of them. But any amusement he'd had didn't last, for one of the magazine's photographs had a peculiar effect on him, a picture he'd found in a spread that featured, a caption indicated, an eighteen-year-old boy named Dano.

He grasped the magazine and lit a cigarette, then located this spread. Dano was naked and, in most of the illustrations, strolling down a hill toward a forest. His penis was circumcised, which, Stephen had observed years before in certain Eastern Europeans he'd been with, was unusual for men of that region. His hair was black, thick and curly, his skin bronzed. Stephen was titillated by all of these images, but none was as intriguing as the picture he liked best, the very same one that affected him strangely.

He turned to that image, the final one in the spread, a picture of Dano standing by a pond in the glen of a woods, evidently the forest he'd been approaching. He was leaning against a tree as a soft light—twilight, Stephen assumed—shone through the trees' branches onto his skin, making it appear even more tanned than it had in the other photos. The fading quality of this light emphasized his ruddy cheeks and glowing skin—his youth—in a manner that Stephen found achingly painful. It made him think of his childhood, of the hours he'd spent in the woods near his family's house, alone. More painful for him, though, was Dano's expression: Well aware of the photographer's presence, he was gazing toward the camera and grinning coyly. The discomfort his smile produced in Stephen was sharp yet almost pleasant, reminding him as it did of Robert as he had appeared the night they'd met, over ten years after Stephen had moved to New York, long before Robert's unsettling despondency set in.

He looked up with a start, picturing Robert as he'd been that night—in a bar, the Triangle, long since closed—clutching a beer and laughing, talking about his attempts to make a career for himself as a painter, which, he'd admitted, had been rather lame. "But, fuck," he told Stephen with a grin, "once I get going…shit, my things are so much better than that crap I see in Soho." Drawn to Robert—by his pretty, sweet face, by his laughter and vivacity—charmed and utterly smitten, Stephen watched him stretch out a hand, form a gun with his fingers, and exclaim, "It'll be like…Bang! That's it, Andy Warhol! Bang! You, too, Mapplethorpe! And you, Julian Schnabel! Bang! You're over!" He smiled flirtatiously as he stroked Stephen's arm. "Even though…" he continued slowly. Then, excited and blushing: "Look, I don't really give a shit about any fucking painting! I mean, you know, it's like there…there're a lot of other things that I…that *we* can do."

Stephen crushed his cigarette in a nearby ashtray, then slugged down all of his wine and filled his glass again. He noticed on the TV that the President of the United States was conducting a press conference. He wondered what that was about. It was six-thirty according to the bedside clock, and the sun outside his window was still quite bright, the room still very hot. He glanced down at the photo of Dano, but couldn't take it in, seeing instead, startlingly, Robert and himself as they'd been years after that first night, shortly before Robert had become ill.

They stood by the couch in the living room, drunk, perhaps stoned as well, arguing about some infidelity, either Robert's or Stephen's, Stephen could no longer remember. "I can't take your shit!" Robert was shouting at Stephen. "Jesus, you're suffocating me!" Enraged—both by this outburst and by the sheer repetition, the monotony of their recent lives—Stephen hesitated for just an instant, then lunged toward Robert, grasping at his throat. "Fucking cunt!" he screamed.

He forced his hands around Robert's neck, squeezing and twisting it. "Fucking little shit!" Sweating, his face now crimson, Robert pulled away, using, it seemed, nearly all of his strength. He took a clumsy, drunken swing at Stephen, but missed. "Don't, you fuck!" he cried. "Don't *ever* fucking touch me again!" He took another swing, feebler this time, missing once more, then ran to the window and, gasping, stared out onto the street. Out of breath, Stephen watched him intently. Robert was trembling.

Stephen tightened his grip on the magazine in his hands and did his best to concentrate on it. Slowly Dano came into focus, first his bronzed skin, then his black hair and lively blue eyes. As Stephen took in the image, he again remembered Robert as he'd been at the Triangle, eager, so young. Stephen had been fairly young then, too, thirty-five—old enough, though, to have tired just a bit of all the meandering he'd done since he'd moved to New York, to have a dim but distinct urge to settle down. Somehow he'd thought that if he did this, it would make his separation from his parents more complete. He'd been looking for someone who would take his mind off himself.

He grabbed another cigarette from his pack, then attempted to compare the fresh-faced Robert of that first night with the depressed and dissipated one he remembered from that fight they'd had years later, the worst of the many they'd been through. He wanted to understand what had occurred in the years between, what had happened to them. He wondered if it had been the result of their getting older, if both he and Robert had grown frustrated with their lives and tired of one another. Gazing down at Dano, he recalled Robert in the last days of his illness, deathly pale, withering away. He quickly glanced up toward the TV and saw the president, still conducting his press conference, which had become animated, with dozens of reporters vying raucously for the president's attention. At that

moment he remembered what it had been like after Robert had died, how shattered he'd felt, and how disoriented.

He'd tried to tell himself then that it wasn't his fault, that Robert would have gotten sick even if they'd been blissfully happy. He'd tried to tell himself that none of this had happened, that Robert was still alive and that they were both still young, that the world hadn't changed. Yet every day, as he walked through the East Village, through their old neighborhood, what he saw gave lie to any hopes he may have had. The world *had* changed, or at any rate seemed completely different from what it had been like when he and Robert had met. He felt as if he'd been oblivious to everything besides themselves during their years together, unaware of what occurred around them. The building at the corner of Norfolk and Houston, the one that had housed the bodega where he and Robert had bought pot, had been renovated and turned into a complex of cooperative apartments. An enormous high-rise was being constructed two blocks from his home. Professional types in business suits or in crisply pressed dresses were common on streets that had once appeared almost exclusively populated by Latinos and bohemians. It felt to Stephen as if everything had passed him by.

But more frightening than anything, he knew now, was the presence of AIDS. He looked at his legs, sticking out from his robe. An inch above his left ankle was a purplish mark, tiny but unmistakably a lesion. He'd been conscious of this for nearly two months, but had said nothing to anyone. It terrified him, and he didn't want to have his fears confirmed by doctors. Besides, he'd let his health insurance lapse after he'd lost his last job, when he couldn't afford to keep up the payments. Cutbacks in social services had drastically reduced all government aid, making it impossible for him to receive assistance. That wouldn't make a difference anyway, he felt. What could anyone do? Give him something that might not even work? Nothing had helped Robert or Peter, not even protease inhibitors or other up-to-date treatments. Why prolong the misery?

He glanced at the magazine he was holding, at Dano, wondering what had gone wrong, what he and Robert could have done differently, if there was something he could have said to make things better. Perhaps it had been the drugs that he and Robert had taken, all their drinking. Or maybe it had been something else.

He remembered how, for a brief period three years after he and Robert had met—when they were fighting a bit but still got along most of the time, and Robert's dark moods had not yet become apparent—he'd consulted a psychotherapist, Ellen, hoping she could help him and Robert sort out some of their problems. During one session, Ellen speculated that— because of Stephen's childhood, with both his parents so narcissistic—forming any sort of healthy relationship was bound to be difficult for him, though he could do so if he worked very hard, and therapy might help.

That night after the session, he and Robert had sex. When they were finished, Stephen felt the way he had after they'd first connected, lazily in love, and, in a burst of candor, told Robert what Ellen had said. Robert seemed touched. He wedged himself against Stephen's back and threw his arms across his chest, murmuring, "Look, you can trust me. Really. I'm not like those shits you grew up with." Stephen was moved and for that moment believed him.

Years later, long after he'd grown tired of Ellen's counseling and had stopped seeing her, when he and Robert fought much more and were frequently unfaithful to each other, he couldn't believe anything Robert said. He felt as if he'd dreamed their good times.

He gulped down the remainder of his wine and poured more into his glass, staring at the TV. The president was continuing his press conference, the muscles in his face taut, making him appear exceedingly serious, even more so than he had a minute earlier. Quickly looking away, Stephen glanced down at Dano's skin, at the twilight streaming onto it.

He thought of a dream he'd had the week before, one of the few things that had made him feel at all hopeful recently. In it, he'd been in his parents' house, on the stairway. At the top of the stairs, just outside his bedroom, was the couch where he used to sit while Ethel read him stories. His cat Rose was lying there, staring at him and purring. Sunlight from an overhead window shone down onto her gray fur and onto the stairway's polished brown banister. Seeing Rose alive again and sensing the bright sunshine around him filled Stephen with an overwhelming joy. The sunlight became much brighter, absorbing him and everything else. He awoke. The joy he'd experienced in his dream stayed with him for an hour or so, until, finally, it was subsumed by his usual despair.

He concentrated on the president's press conference. He felt drunk and his vision was blurry, but he could tell that the president was speaking heatedly, and his hands appeared to be shaking. His own hands were shaking as well. He couldn't imagine what was going on.

A reporter asked a question, and the president seemed to falter. Stephen thought that he detected an elusive panic in his eyes, which reminded him of Robert in one of his blacker moods, when he'd lie awake in bed for hours, saying nothing. These moods had frustrated Stephen, infuriated him, too, but he'd understood them: He often felt like that. It seemed to him at those times as if he and Robert could have been one.

"Move your ass!" a man on the street shouted, and Stephen lowered his eyes. He tried to focus on the photo of Dano, then thought of his dream again, of the joy he'd felt in it, of the sunlight. He recalled being in the woods near his parents' house, standing by the pond there. It was a summer evening around seven and very hot, exactly like it was today, and he'd gone to the woods to escape a party his parents were giving. He could hear crickets chirping nearby and found the sounds they made soothing, just as he did the smell of the moist grass beneath him. He loved being alone like this. Over a hill, yards away, he heard Ethel calling from his parents' house: "Stevie! Stevie, honey, come home! It's dinner time, baby!" He paid no attention to her; he knew she wouldn't be angry. He wanted to linger here for just a bit longer, take in the light as the sun began to set. He wanted to make this time last.

He yawned, suddenly sleepy, feeling sad and oppressively lonely. It occurred to him then that when he'd met Robert, he'd been longing for moments such as the one he'd just recalled. But hadn't he experienced many such moments with Robert? For a few years anyway? He wanted to remember more of them, think about how they used to lie in bed together, their legs entwined, but found it difficult to do so. He glanced up, past the image of the president on the TV, through his bedroom's doorway, at the window in the living room—the very spot where Robert had stood that day, his back to Stephen, trembling after their fight. He remembered the anger he'd felt, especially when he'd seen Robert raise his hands to his face and heard him sobbing. "Little fuck!" Stephen had screamed at him. "Piece of shit! I hope you fucking die!" Robert froze, but said nothing. He did not turn around or even look back.

Stephen poured the last of the wine into his glass and finished it off. The sun was a good deal lower in the sky but still seemed too bright, and the apartment was hideously hot. He felt old and parched, in need of whatever it was that Robert had given him when they'd met, whatever had helped ease some of the painful memories he had—at least for a while, during his and Robert's good years. Robert's dead, he reminded himself; it's been three years today. He could never reclaim what they'd had.

He tossed the magazine onto the floor and stretched out on the bed. He wished he could live his life over, do something to redeem it. His vision became blurrier, though he could still see the president on the TV, blathering, it appeared, desperately. He looked downward, dizzy, and felt as if he would soon pass out. He saw something on the floor, a pamphlet, "Rejoice in the Night to Come." His heart throbbed madly. "The Rapture," he mumbled aloud, much more alert, then alarmed. A passage from the Bible was printed on the pamphlet's cover: "And at that time shall Michael stand up, the great prince which standeth for the children of the people." As he read this, the pace of his heartbeat slowed. He sensed something within himself, a peculiar sort of calm. This feeling stayed with him. He drifted off.

Through the light surrounding him, he could see Rose awake on the couch, and he knew that he was a child once more. He saw that he was part of the light and that he was floating. There was something directly above him that he'd wanted to find, a beautiful form, a boy. He reached up toward him, and the telephone rang. He tried to clutch the boy's hand, and the phone rang again. The boy smiled down at him. The phone rang a third time. Then he heard Sharon's voice coming through the speaker of his answering machine. Her tone was agitated: "Stephen, come on, pick up! I know you're there! I can't believe everything that's going on, what they're saying on the news."

Half asleep, he grabbed the phone. "What's that?"

Sharon answered, relieved: "Oh, Stephen, thank God! It's so crazy what's happening. I'm really scared."

He tried to rouse himself and make sense of what Sharon was saying. Groggy and still high, he looked toward the TV.

The newscasters he'd seen before were back on, along with three other commentators. Everyone looked worried.

"You're watching, aren't you?" Sharon asked him. "The news?"

He stared at the grim faces of the TV commentators, then glanced at the clock by his bed. It was five past nine. He turned toward the living room. It appeared unusually bright in there for this time of the evening. "N…no."

"Jesus," Sharon exclaimed excitedly, "there's something going on in Russia. I mean, Petrovitch sent all these troops to Chechnya's border and then…they don't know why, but we lost contact with them. Everything over there just went blank. They're afraid of what that maniac might have done."

Stephen could barely comprehend what Sharon was saying. He kept his attention fixed on the brightness in the living room, then recognized it as that light, the light from his dream. He felt very hot and was perspiring.

"I can't believe you haven't heard anything," Sharon continued. "That's all they're talking about on TV."

Slowly the light began to fade, and he noticed someone by the living room window, a man.

"Come on, Stephen, say something. I'm terrified."

He realized it was Robert, turning from the window toward him.

"Stephen? Are you there? Please, talk to me!"

He gripped the phone and took a long breath, gazing at Robert. "I…I've gotta go," he gasped.

"No, Stephen, don't! My parents aren't around, and I…I need to hear your voice. That shit in Russia's really freaking me out."

"*Please*," he answered, shaking. "Later, okay?" He threw the phone down onto the cradle.

Still standing by the window in the next room, Robert smiled at him. He didn't seem emaciated at all, as he had when he'd been sick. Nor did he appear depressed and dissipated.

He looked boyishly young, exuberantly happy, exactly like he'd looked when they'd met. His smile grew wider.

It felt to Stephen as if after all these years, all the time that had passed since that fight, that Robert had turned from the window at last. He kept his eyes locked on Robert's and was sure that what he saw was real, that Robert actually was there. Oh, God, Robert, he thought. Shit, *Bobbie*. He wanted to run to the living room, throw his arms around Robert and make things right.

Before Stephen could do anything, Robert raised a hand and opened his mouth. The words he spoke were silent, but Stephen heard them clearly. "Not yet," Robert said, then dispersed into the air and was gone.

The phone started ringing again. Stephen jumped up from his bed and hurried into the living room to the window, to the same spot where Robert had stood.

Sharon's voice shot out of the answering machine in the bedroom: "Stephen, what's going on? What happened to you? What's the matter? Come on, talk to me!"

He stared out the window. It was dark now, and there was a strange tint to the sky, brightly orange yet unlike any color he'd ever seen. Hundreds of stars were visible, unusual for the city, and he noticed an airplane above the bright skyline over Queens, heading for Kennedy Airport, he supposed. Far away he heard a helicopter.

"All right," Sharon sighed from the answering machine. "I don't know what you're doing, but I guess I'll go. Call me back as soon as you can, okay?" She hesitated for a second, then hung up.

He looked down at the street. A great many people were on the sidewalk. He focused on the group of boys he'd seen by the curb earlier. There were more of them there now. A radio was blasting news. "The president is meeting with his cabinet," a male announcer said gravely. "We'll keep you posted throughout the night as events develop."

Stephen glanced to the right of the boys. Charlene was standing close to them, wearing her faded green dress. Stunned, he backed away from the window. She peered up toward him. For a second he wondered what had happened to her mother and Timothy. Then he heard one word, "Raptured," spoken in a young girl's voice. He leaned forward and again looked at

Charlene, thinking it was she who had spoken. He remembered then that she was mute, and she grinned—at him, he was sure.

A song came on the radio outside: "I like you, baby. I like you a lot." His eyes on Charlene, on her smiling, calm face, Stephen recalled something that he thought Timothy had said to him, something about Robert: "He's with God, like so many others. But he'll only be away for a little while longer." A sense of exhilaration swept through him, and he began swaying to the beat of the song. He moved away from the window and started dancing.

"Yeah, I like my baby a lot."

He stopped. What he saw—the gray couch by the wall, a Matisse print hanging directly above it, the old rug on the floor, all exactly where they had been for years and years— appeared sterile. He didn't want to be inside any longer; he hadn't gone out at all for days. He felt expectant, anticipatory, just as he had so much of the time when he was young. He wanted to be out in the night.

"Oh, yeah, I like you."

He heard the helicopter coming closer, toward his apartment building. He stood completely still, frightened by its sound. He wished he had more wine, though he knew that he was already drunk.

"Take my hand if you like me, too."

He looked toward the window and saw the orangish tint in the sky. He found it beautiful and thought of Robert.

"I like you, I like you, I like you so much."

He started swaying once more, heading toward his closet and opening its door, grabbing a lightweight blue shirt and a pair of jeans from their hangers. He threw off his robe, let it drop to the floor, and pulled the shirt and jeans on. He put a hand in the right pocket of his pants and found a twenty-dol-

lar bill, the only money he'd have until his next unemployment check arrived. What the fuck? he thought; you only live once.

He darted out of the living room, through his bedroom, to the apartment's front door. Once there he paused, uncertain.

"I got you, I got you. Oh, yeah, I got you, baby!"

He felt a new burst of energy and rushed out the door.

3

As soon as Stephen left his building, he couldn't imagine what had come over him. It was even hotter than it had been in his apartment, and an extraordinarily large number of people was milling about, many more than he'd noticed from his window, than he normally would see outside on a Sunday night. All appeared to be in an animated, even festive mood, and most were clearly high. He mulled the possibility that the events in Russia might have unleashed something they hadn't known existed, that some sort of tension they'd all felt was unravelling. Then he wondered if he, too, were losing it; he had, after all, thought he'd seen Robert inside. That just couldn't be.

Memories of the day cascaded through his head: the Children of Michael; Timothy, Ruth, and Charlene; the possible outbreak of war. Everything felt off, disorienting, like something from his childhood—moments when he was very young, before his impressions of his mother and father and of Ethel had been completely formed—or like the first months after Robert had died, when his world, what he'd known, had collapsed.

He looked toward the group of boys he'd watched from his apartment and saw that Charlene was gone. He felt terrified by this and by what was happening, by the crowd on the street, the heat, and the strange tint of the sky. Yet he couldn't bring himself to go back upstairs; he felt compelled to move on.

A helicopter hovered far above him, beaming down lights, which were searching a vacant lot to his left. More terrified, he sped in the direction of Avenue A. He didn't know what he wanted to do. He considered going to some club, though his last experience at a club had not been a pleasant one. It had been at a jerk-off bar in the West Village, one of a number of such places that had opened since AIDS had arisen and safer-sex guidelines had been established, and it had been crowded, most of its patrons middle-aged men, many of them flabby, all naked or wearing just underpants. The sight of these men embracing, clinging together as they jerked each other off, only served to remind Stephen of how old he was. He stayed for less than ten minutes.

Perspiring, he reached Avenue A and saw that it was even more densely packed with pedestrians here than it had been on his block. Most of them were young, hurrying past Stephen and speaking in lively, loud voices. An elderly man with thin gray hair and a cane inched his way downtown, and it occurred to Stephen that it wouldn't be long before he was that old himself—if, of course, he didn't get sick and die first. Stopping abruptly, he pulled a cigarette from the pack in his pocket. The air seemed strangely electric, and he felt light-headed and very warm, feverish. He wondered if he was reacting to the heat and the day's events, or if this was something else, if he was getting sick.

Two men in their early twenties pushed through the crowd and sauntered by. "Come on, Mike," the taller one screamed gleefully to the second, "you know they've been nuked!"

Stephen saw that both were good-looking, in a clean-cut, collegiate way that wasn't appealing to him. He assumed they were university students living in a dorm that had been built a few months ago on East 6th Street. He'd seen a lot of these students in the neighborhood recently. All seemed very different from the people he'd gone to school with in the early seventies, when the world, he thought, had been more relaxed, the friends he'd had adventurous and curious. The students he'd observed lately appeared to him prematurely ambitious and, as they hurried from class to class, neurotically focused for their age, to be moving much too decisively. At night, though, many partied rowdily, with an almost ruthless determination that he found a little frightening. He was sure he'd never been like that, like they appeared to him, boorishly loud and insensitive.

"Yeah, you're right," the second man replied, his tone just as gleeful as his friend's. "Those fuckers are dead." Both rushed on, laughing uproariously.

Stephen stood still, holding the unlit cigarette. Sweat streamed across his brow and from under his arms, and despite the intense heat, he was shivering. He became convinced that he was ill and considered returning home and crawling back into bed. But he wanted a drink. Any old dive would do, just to have a few quick ones.

He walked north, through the throngs that congested every block. At the corner on 5th Street, he noticed a ragged person whom he recognized, a blond boy in his mid-teens, dreadlocked and wearing filthy clothes, panhandling. At first he couldn't recall where he'd seen him before. Then he remembered: It had been at a fire he'd witnessed in February, around ten blocks from his apartment building, a suspicious one, according to an article he'd later read in the *Village Voice*, for it had destroyed two adjoining buildings illegally occupied by squatters, with circumstances indicating it could very well have been set by the buildings' owner.

It had happened at six on a Saturday evening. Stephen had been ambling home, drunk, having spent the afternoon in a bar, when he saw fire trucks and ambulances speeding noisily uptown. Startled, he worried that they could be going to his block—although, he then realized, they were heading in the

opposite direction. He followed them to 7th Street. There he found the two buildings in flames, fire and smoke shooting toward the dark, overcast sky as an immense crowd watched from across the street, at least thirty of the squatters among them, young men, women, and a few children, shivering in the cold, smoky air. Many were dreadlocked or with multicolored hair, and all were sooty and distressed. Nearly a dozen dogs, gnarled mongrels, frisked agitatedly around the squatters, barking. Most of the dogs were covered with dirty blankets, which had been used as makeshift coats. A pink-haired woman in a tie-dyed robe sat cross-legged on the ground, her eyes downcast. She glanced up, staring at the burning buildings. "Shit!" she cried. "Oh, *shit!*" Stephen followed her gaze. A blond teenage boy in a baggy pair of boxer shorts was trapped on the fourth-floor fire escape of the easternmost building. Flames shot out of a window a few feet to his right, and he was standing frozen. One of the fire trucks had a ladder raised, and a fireman was climbing it frantically, attempting to rescue the boy. But the smoke around them was thick, and any chance of the boy escaping seemed unlikely. Stephen imagined him having to jump, landing on the pavement with a splat. "Shit!" the pink-haired woman cried again. "Jesus, fuck!" The dogs barked more loudly. A cold gust of wind blew past Stephen, and he took a deep breath, then felt smoke enter his lungs. He coughed. His head was pounding, his heart as well. He turned quickly and dashed home.

Somehow the boy had survived. Standing now in front of Stephen, he stared ahead imploringly, his eyes a vacant blue. Stephen caught a hint of fear on his pale face, a reminder of the terror he'd observed there that February night. He felt heat careening toward his head and sweat streaming down his chest. He couldn't look at the boy any longer and, dropping his cigarette on the ground, peered at the sky. The orangish tint was still there, as well as the innumerable stars, and he could feel once more a faint electricity in the air. He lowered his eyes. Just behind the boy, standing next to a packed delicatessen, in the midst of the crowd outside, an olive-skinned woman was handing a pamphlet to a long-haired man passing by. "Have you heard about Michael?" she asked in a British accent as he took it from her. "He's here." Stephen was able to make out the pamphlet's title, "Rejoice in the Night to Come." He sucked in his breath and moved his eyes back to the boy's ashen face. Another wave of heat surged through him, and he thought that he might faint.

A group of teenagers stumbled by drunkenly. "Fucking Russians!" one shouted. "The bastards!"

The woman with the pamphlets approached Stephen, holding one toward him. He looked away, up at the sky, then down toward a bar to the left of the delicatessen. It was called Muffin, and he remembered reading or hearing about it somewhere, about how it had drag shows on Thursday nights and go-go boys on Fridays and Saturdays.

"Michael's here!" the woman gushed at him. "Our wait is over!"

Another group pushed by, two girls and a boy, all giggling.

"No thanks!" Stephen cried to the woman, then, impulsively, ran to Muffin's door, rushing inside.

It took his eyes several moments to adjust to the club's interior, since it was dimly lit, with only flickering fluorescent lights, painted a deep forest green, running across the tall ceiling and around the bar at the end of the long room. The club was air-conditioned and very cold, and North African music was playing, the same music, Stephen realized, that he had heard at his friend Peter's apartment one night years ago, a man and a woman chanting words to a song that was, Peter had told him, a prime example of Algerian pop-rai. As Stephen's eyes grew used to the light, he saw that the room was nearly empty. Three handsome men in dark clothing, black T-shirts and pants, stood by a jukebox to his right. A middle-

aged man and woman sat at a round table several yards in front of them. At the bar, sitting alone, a black-haired boy in tight jeans talked to the muscular, tattooed bartender.

Stephen stood still. The emptiness of the club seemed eerie yet horribly familiar, like his life, the emptiness he felt so much of the time. He remained by the entryway, unsure what to do.

Above the din of the music, he heard the high-pitched voice of the woman at the round table, speaking to the man by her side. "All of this would be pretty upsetting to me, you know, George," she said brightly. "I mean, it would be if I weren't so blissed out on my anti-depressants."

A frigid blast from the air-conditioner blew past Stephen. Shivering, he stared at the two of them. The woman was tall, buxom, and blonde, and was wearing a tight, black-and-white checkered dress; George, reed-thin, with thick red-framed glasses, a light blue sports jacket, and green shorts. Stephen thought that he'd seen a photograph of him on the contributors' page of *Vanity Fair*. He didn't appear to be paying attention to anything the woman said: His head was angled away from her, toward the boy at the bar.

Stephen studied the boy, too. He was leaning over the bar's counter toward the bartender, and his bright red T-shirt had risen from the waist of his pants, revealing an expanse of tanned skin at his lower back. Stephen couldn't see his face, but his black hair was very thick, and Stephen suspected he was sexy. He looked to his right and saw that the three handsome men were also gazing at the boy, whispering and laughing.

The beat of the Algerian music grew more frantic, and the Arabic words came more rapidly. Again the blonde woman's voice could be heard above the song: "Hell, George, maybe I should just have a nervous breakdown and get it over with."

Stephen wanted a drink desperately. He started toward the bar, the muscles in his back tense. As he walked past the three handsome men, he could hear them giggling and thought they were laughing at him. "The cow!" one of them shrieked. "What a silly fucking cunt!"

He increased his pace and reached the bar, then stopped, his eyes on the back of the boy, first on his thick black hair, then on the patch of tanned skin visible below his T-shirt.

Suddenly the boy swerved around and grinned at him.

"Hey," he cried, as if recognizing Stephen. "I haven't run into *you* in a while."

Stephen was jarred, certain that he'd never before met this boy. He saw that he was indeed very sexy; his black hair and bronzed skin emphasized his eyes, which were brown and glistening, vapid yet strangely morose, sad. He thought of the night that he'd met Robert at the Triangle and was sure something like that could never happen now: He was middle-aged. He didn't know what to say.

"Come on, sit down," the boy continued, his words slurred, his tone bleary but very provocative. "I was just talking to Ron here." He motioned toward the muscular bartender and, more seductively, added, "He was telling me about how he was going to fist me later tonight."

Ron smiled and clenched the fingers of his right hand into a tight ball. "Yeah," he said. His voice was raspy and eager. "I'll shove it right up your sweet little hole." Leering, he spoke to Stephen: "This fucker Davey'll take anything on."

Stephen felt unnerved. Davey appeared to be flirting with him, yet that seemed to him unlikely, unattractive as he thought himself. He suspected that Davey's interest might be feigned, a put-on, and tried to concentrate on one of the tattoos on Ron's right arm, a bluish crab with an opened, fierce-looking claw. He wanted to order a drink, but was unable to utter a word.

"Shit, sit down, okay?" Davey pinched Stephen's left buttock, then grabbed his waist and pulled him onto a seat beside him. He winked at Ron. "Ron'll buy you a drink. He's not making any money now anyway. It sucks here tonight. No one's around."

"That's 'cause of those fucks in Russia," Ron muttered angrily. "Everyone's freaked."

Stephen turned in his seat and glanced behind him. Nearly all of the others in the room appeared to be looking at them, the three handsome men still giggling, the blonde woman gazing with adoration at George as he peered toward the bar, watching Davey. The Algerian woman on the CD was singing another song, one that sounded like a dirge. Stephen moved his eyes back to Davey and noticed that he had a hand on the crotch of his jeans and was fondling himself. He stared at Ron, who was eyeing Davey lecherously.

The woman on the CD wailed.

"Jesus fucking Christ, that fucking rag head!" Ron exclaimed. He pointed at the three men laughing in the distance. "Those faggots over there put that shit on. I'm gonna go change it." He lurched out from behind the bar and started toward the jukebox. "Play some c&w, or some fucking rock 'n' roll."

Davey looked at Stephen and gestured toward the departing Ron. "A real brute, right?" he said, a gleam in his eyes, then giggled.

Stephen watched Ron approach the jukebox, observing, too, the others in the room. Their eyes were still focused in his direction, on Davey, even the blonde woman, who had shifted her attention from George. He turned back to Davey and saw that he was grinning at him, that his hand remained on his crotch, and that he had an erection.

"I told you, didn't I," Davey asked him, speaking slowly, his voice languid and more distant, "what my father did to me when I was a kid?"

With a start, Stephen leaned back in his seat, looking toward the rows of bottles on the shelf behind the bar, wishing Ron would return. He wanted to order a drink. "What...what are you talking about?"

"Oh, you *know*," Davey answered coyly. "I mean, I'm sure I told you all about *that*."

Stephen lit a cigarette, noticing how unsteady his hand was. "But this is the first time we've met," he mumbled. He

glanced away and saw Ron leaning over the jukebox, then looked back at Davey.

"Come on, don't be *stupid*." Davey unzipped his pants and slipped a hand inside them. "You fucked me in the back of that limo."

Stephen drew deeply on his cigarette. For a second he wondered if he had forgotten about something, some incident with Davey. Maybe he'd been drunk and blacked out. He doubted that, though. He would have remembered someone as good-looking as Davey. He suspected once more that Davey was putting him on, that this was a hoax.

"I want a drink," he muttered to Davey, under his breath.

Davey removed his hand from his pants and jumped up. "Sure," he cried and, using his hands as levers, pulled himself over the bar. "What'll it be?" He grabbed a bottle of scotch and two glasses from the bar's shelf. "Is this okay?"

Stephen's eyes were on Davey's crotch, and he could see that his jeans were still unzipped and, beneath the denim, that he was still erect. "Yeah, that's fine," he answered distractedly.

A song by Motley Crüe came on, and Ron began dancing by the jukebox, gyrating wildly while flinging his long, muscular arms back and forth.

Davey placed the bottle and glasses on the counter, then hopped back over the bar. He sat next to Stephen, allowing a leg to rest against his, filled the two glasses with scotch, and took a slug from one of them. Stephen grasped the second glass and took a slug as well.

Davey reached into a pocket of his pants. His zipper parted slightly, and Stephen caught a glimpse of his black pubic hair.

Davey drew two large, grayish-white pills from his pocket. "You want one of these?" he asked.

Stephen raised his eyes, studying the pills. "What are they?"

"Oh, you know." Davey smiled. "X."

Stephen glanced toward the jukebox. Ron was twirling in circles, flailing his arms ever more wildly. The others in the room were still watching Davey. Stephen looked at him and noted his smile, how thick and sensuous his lips appeared. He wanted to smile back, to give in to the moment, to what he was experiencing, to the mood of the room, to act as he'd done when he was young.

"So, you feel like X-ing?" Davey murmured.

Stephen paused. Then, quickly: "Sure, why not?" He took another slug of his drink. "I mean, what the fuck?"

Davey handed him a pill, and they both swallowed one, finishing their drinks.

Davey poured more scotch into their glasses. "Listen," he said with a grin, speaking abruptly, his voice lethargic. "Later on I want you to take me back to your apartment. I want you to rip off my clothes and tie me to your bed, then take pictures of me. After that you can fuck me."

Stephen crushed his cigarette in an ashtray, trembling with desire and fear. This kid's nuts, he told himself. Despite the room's air-conditioning, he was sweating. He wiped his brow, for an instant unable to look at Davey. He tried to think of something to say and glanced up. Davey's black hair and tanned skin seemed too black and too tanned, his broad smile cruel. But Stephen was still tantalized. "Aren't... aren't I...?"

"Yeah?" Davey stroked Stephen's arm.

"Well, aren't I a little old for you?"

Davey laughed. "Oh, *please*! Old is good!" He grabbed Stephen's stomach, tweaking a roll of fat. "The older and fatter the better."

Stephen felt his face turning red. He wanted to disappear.

Davey kept his hand at Stephen's waist, playing with the fat there. "At least let me suck you off."

Stephen glanced behind him. The three handsome men seemed to be moving closer. He glanced back at Davey.

Davey put a hand in his pants and pulled out his penis. It was long and erect. He rubbed it. "So what about you?" he asked Stephen. "Let me see your cock."

Stephen again looked behind him. The three men were definitely moving closer now. Both George and the blonde woman appeared to be watching the proceedings with great interest. Motley Crüe was still playing, but Ron had stopped dancing and was watching as well.

Davey turned toward the others and shouted, "Come on! I'll do you all." He gulped the rest of his drink, then poured more scotch into his and Stephen's glasses.

The three men hurried toward the bar, Ron, too. George and the woman continued to watch.

Stephen stared at Davey, again observing how his eyes appeared morose, somehow dead. He looked away, at the bottles lined up on the bar, and tried to convince himself that he was having fun, that this was the way things had been in the seventies, that he was about to relive his youth. He was unable to do so. He looked back toward Davey and saw Ron and the three handsome men draw up beside him. They pulled their penises out. Davey started blowing the tallest of them, a dark-skinned man with short, bleached hair. Shit, Stephen thought, this isn't like the seventies. It didn't feel buoyant like those days had. It felt like a nightmare. He took a gulp of scotch, wondering when the pill that Davey had given him would kick in.

Davey moved on to the next man, a round-faced, cherubic-looking redhead with a malicious grin. He took his penis in his mouth.

The redhead gripped his head. "Come on, you little slut," he cried, yanking his hair, "you can do better than that."

Davey worked frenetically, hardly gagging at all.

In spite of the room's chill, Stephen felt overcome by heat. He drew his eyes from Davey and looked toward George and the blonde woman. George was leaning forward in his seat, as if about to rise, and the woman was smiling at him benevolently, with, it appeared, total understanding. The song playing on the jukebox ended, and for a moment there was silence.

"Oh, go on," the woman chirped to George, "knock yourself out."

George stood and beamed at her, then sped toward the bar, toward Stephen, to Davey, his pale thin legs prominent under his green shorts, his light blue sports jacket also conspicuous.

As George arrived breathlessly at the bar, Stephen heard the twang of a guitar and the tinkling of a piano. A song by Cheryl Paul, a country-and-western singer, was playing:

If you're going to leave,
do it now and forget me.
Just hurt me, hurt me bad,
if you're going to leave.

Davey pulled away from the redhead and, even more energetically, began blowing Ron.

Stephen glanced off. In the distance, beneath the green, flickering fluorescent lights, he saw the blonde woman sitting at her table. She seemed miles away, completely alone, yet was smiling in his direction, at George, who was standing beside him, gazing with longing at Davey and Ron.

"So you want it?" Ron shouted, pulling his penis out of Davey's mouth and slapping it against his cheek. "You really want it bad, don't you, faggot?"

Davey nodded and again took hold of Ron's penis, resuming his exertions with an increased vigor.

Stephen concentrated on Cheryl Paul's song:

Just leave me all alone,
with my pain, with my shattered dreams.
Just hurt me, just forget me.
I'll never fall in love again.

He felt a hand on his groin and looked downward, seeing Davey.

"It's your turn now," Davey said to him and smiled.

Davey's touch felt unsettlingly cold to Stephen, and he drew away. The room appeared to be dissolving, melting as the green light on the ceiling flickered ominously, and Davey's face seemed red like his shirt, melting as well. Stephen's heart was pumping wildly. He turned and ran, away from Davey, Ron, George, and the three handsome men, toward the bar's entryway, past the woman at her table.

"Hey, where're you going?" Davey called to him.

Stephen kept moving. A big grin on her face, the woman waved at him. He glanced away from her, back toward the bar. Davey had focused on George and was unzipping his green shorts.

Stephen sped to the entryway, pushed the front door open, and ran outside. As he stood on the sidewalk, he felt overwhelmed by the night's hot, sticky air and by the crowd around him, which was even larger than it had been earlier, almost everyone rushing by, as if afraid to keep still. The boy who'd been panhandling was on the corner where he'd stood, and the woman with the pamphlets was still in front of the delicatessen. The sky was much more orange than it had appeared before, fluorescently bright and clear, and there were hundreds, perhaps thousands, of stars visible, shooting stars now. A lone plane flew beneath them. No one besides Stephen seemed to notice any of this, except the woman with the pamphlets, who was pointing toward the sky and screaming, "For then shall be great tribulation, such as was not from the beginning of the world to this time…" Heedless of her and of the sky, the crowd hurried on, only Stephen, the woman, and the panhandler immobile.

Just then Stephen was startled by a shrill voice shouting out to him from a few feet away: "*Stephen*! Stephen Schaeffer!" He spun around. It was Christopher Lawrence, someone he'd known in the eighties and hadn't liked much. Christopher had once had a short affair with Peter, and it seemed to Stephen that Robert, too, had slept with him a few times— although, he considered, maybe it had been he himself who had done so.

Christopher sidled up to him and said, "Christ, Stevie, imagine running into *you*! On tonight of all nights! It's been years!"

Stephen stared at him. He was swaying erratically, his face was red, and he reeked of alcohol. It was obvious that he was stoned, as high as Stephen was, as practically everyone else on

the street seemed to be. Stephen could see that he'd lost a great deal of weight since the last time he'd seen him, that, indeed, he was much too thin, as emaciated as Peter. He was also struck by how old he appeared, his hair, which had been thick, wavy, and blond, now sparse and gray, his once-handsome face wrinkled and drawn. "How…? I…"

Christopher laughed. "Jesus, you look like shit! I mean you've really let yourself go. You used to be so fit."

Stephen felt currents of electricity in the air, much stronger than those he'd felt earlier. He glanced over Christopher's shoulder at the boy panhandling, then, seeing how forlorn and terrified he was, peered up at the countless shooting stars. Alarmed, he looked downward and to his side. He noticed someone, a child, wearing a faded green dress, turning sharply around the corner on 5th Street, walking quickly, heading west. Though he couldn't see her face, he could tell she was Charlene. He wondered if she knew what was happening. She disappeared before he could go to her.

Two firecrackers exploded across the street, and Christopher chuckled. "I can't believe this crap, all the shit going down. It's unreal."

A third firecracker went off, its sound deafening. A group of teenage girls passed by, whispering to each other and giggling.

Stephen stared at Christopher's flushed face, into his red eyes. "What…like…What's going on? I mean…Is there any news from Russia? Has something happened over there?" A fourth firecracker exploded. As it did, Stephen thought that he saw the sky open up, the orange parting to give way to more shooting stars, seemingly millions of them, some golden, others a light blue.

Christopher gaped at Stephen. "What's that? You haven't heard?" He shook his head. "I can't believe it! But then, I guess you always were a space cadet."

Stephen wanted at that moment to be at his apartment, to be with Robert. He wanted to feel safe, like he'd felt before everything changed, changed into something unfamiliar, strange, and frightening.

"Having eyes, see ye not?" screamed the woman with the pamphlets, still pointing toward the sky. "And having ears, hear ye not? And do ye not remember?"

The boy who was panhandling cringed.

Weaving precariously, Christopher laughed. "Yeah, the

Ukrainians really did it this time. Surprised the shit out of the Russians while they were busy in Chechnya. Those sly fuckers dropped a couple of bombs on Moscow around an hour ago."

Stephen gazed at the sky, now a solid mass of gold and blue stars. Christopher's words made no sense to him.

The woman with the pamphlets continued to point upward. "For it will be a unique day which is known to the Lord," she shouted, "neither day nor night."

The boy who'd been panhandling turned eastward and ran.

"I...I don't understand," Stephen said to Christopher, his voice faint and unsteady, his eyes on the sky.

"Come on, Stevie, get it together!" Christopher smiled. "Moscow's been nuked."

The woman continued shouting: "But it will all come about that at evening time there will be light."

An immense golden comet shot across the sky, dominating everything.

"Don't you see?" Christopher cried, cackling.

"What?" Stephen was shaking.

"Jesus, Stevie!" Christopher laughed more raucously. A second, more golden comet appeared in the sky. "Shit, it's the fucking end of the world!"

PART II
MICHAEL

I

Three days after Moscow was bombed, Stephen caught a song he'd never heard coming up to his apartment from the street. The recording was called "Moment of Pain" and was by a popular star named Fidelity, a tall and reedy, prettily effeminate man with a distinct falsetto voice, one Stephen recognized immediately. Fidelity sang of a love he'd lost years before and of a hope he'd had that had expired as well. He sang of people who had died and of those he'd never see again, with a bitter rasp to his tone, so that the song seemed sardonic. The words he sang were melancholy yet peculiarly funny and were addressed, Stephen was sure, to people much younger than himself, all of whom considered themselves as worldly as Fidelity appeared to be and who felt just as knowing as he evidently did.

Such were Stephen's thoughts, at any rate, when he heard the song for the second time that day, thinking then, too, that this could well become one of those tunes he'd hear everywhere. It was just before five in the afternoon, and he was on the telephone with Sharon, not really listening. She had called to ask what had happened to him the last time they'd spoken, why he'd hung up. Stephen had almost forgotten about their aborted conversation; much had occurred in the time that had ensued, and the parameters of the world had changed. He found it nearly impossible to sleep much—though he'd been mostly inert by the TV since his night at Muffin's.

"Hey, Stephen, are you there?" Sharon asked him, her tone self-consciously light, it seemed to him, at least when compared to the perturbation that had clouded her voice a few seconds before. "You're acting kind of out of it."

"Oh, well…Look, I'm sorry." Fatigued, Stephen pulled a cigarette from his pack. "I guess it's hard for me to focus on anything today."

"I know what you're talking about." Sharon's voice again sounded troubled. "I feel that way, too, with all the shit going on. And my father's got that flu. I'm pretty worried about him. Everything's been fucked."

"Yeah. And in this heat."

The temperature that afternoon was in the low hundreds for the fifth straight day, the twelfth time that summer it had gotten so high. It hadn't been below ninety for nearly two months. Newspapers had reported numerous deaths in the city due to the oppressive combination of heat and humidity. But the weather was not the primary cause of Stephen's indolence. Instead, central to his inertia were the events he'd seen unfolding on TV, on news updates that were broadcast frequently.

Fidelity's voice floated up from outside. "A moment of pain," he sang with a weary brightness. "Yes, a moment of pain. It came to an end in a moment of pain."

Uneasy, Sharon observed, "It's strange, being with my parents right now, with what's happening. I feel so out of touch. You know, with anything real, with my friends."

Stephen glanced toward the muted TV. A game show was playing, one designed for singles in their late teens and early twenties. Six young men in tight bathing suits paraded past a young, dark-haired woman in a bikini. She was sitting on a throne, and the point of the game was for her to choose the man she wanted to date by grabbing him as he passed. Stephen found this program mindless, yet far preferable to what had been on TV earlier: reports of the war, of nuclear weapons going off in Russia, Chechnya, and Ukraine; seemingly endless clips of terrified refugees crossing borders; harrowing tales of the devastation and radiation present over there; warnings about the threat of fallout spreading further, throughout Asia and Europe. He didn't want to think about any of this. The game show's inanity was welcome.

"Listen," Sharon inquired abruptly, "have you heard from Peter?"

Stephen took a long drag on his cigarette. He wished she hadn't asked that question. He kept his eyes on the TV. The woman in the bikini grasped a beefy blond man, and he sat on her lap. "No. No, nothing," Stephen mumbled.

"*What?*"

"Nothing at all."

Sharon hesitated. Then, worried, she said, "You've tried calling him, haven't you?"

Stephen watched as the woman in the bikini nuzzled the blond man's neck. "A lot, all the time. A few times every day. There's never any answer."

"God, Stephen, something must be wrong! I mean, I've tried calling him, too, and…Shit, where could he be? He's so sick. Maybe you should go over there."

Stephen found Sharon's words, her distressed, emotional voice, worrisome. He gazed at the TV. The woman in the bikini and the blond man were kissing as the show's credits rolled. "Well, maybe I will," he muttered. An edge to his tone, he added, "But look, there're a lot of things I've gotta do right now. I better hang up."

"I should go, too, I guess. But really, stop by Peter's. Tonight if you can, okay?"

"Don't worry." Stephen became more aware of the slight fever he had, a constant, frightening presence since his night at Muffin's. He wiped his brow.

"I'll call you tomorrow." Sharon paused. Then: "You *will* go to Peter's, won't you?"

"Come on, don't you trust me?"

"Sure I do. I just want to make sure." Sharon produced a thin laugh, one that was clearly forced. "So I'll talk to you."

"Yeah. Yeah, right, we'll talk."

"Bye then."

"Bye." Stephen dropped the phone onto its cradle, sweating more heavily, hearing Fidelity's voice lilting upward from outside: "That moment of pain lasted forever. She's gone, and it's here to stay. It'll never go away."

He lay on his bed, fully clothed, frustrated by Sharon's request. She'd reminded him of his own worries about Peter, expressed what he'd only considered then put out of his mind.

He felt unexpectedly like he had one evening two years ago, when he and Sharon had gone to a bar near his apartment, one popular with NYU students. On that night, after eyeing some attractive young men, Stephen had studied Sharon, comparing her face with those of the students sitting nearby. She appeared to him unmistakably middle-aged, her formerly brown hair almost completely gray, her wrinkles deep and prominent. He knew at that moment that he appeared middle-aged himself, to Sharon and to the men he saw, to everyone else in the room. He was very disturbed, furious with Sharon for making him see this; it had never before struck him so strongly. He left the bar immediately, ran home, and went to bed. He was unable to sleep at all.

Now, like then, his alarm was palpable. Sharon was right, though, he decided. Peter wasn't answering his phone, and that seemed ominous. He could only imagine the worst.

He stared at the TV, which was showing the five o'clock news, and saw a church in Los Angeles, its walls crumbling, the result of a small earthquake that had occurred there earlier that day. He attempted to dismiss what he saw, tell himself that it was just more shit. Yesterday it had been the disappearance of two planes, one in Thailand, the other in Bolivia, making it twenty that had vanished thus far this month. He continued gazing at the television screen, watching a dozen women scavenge in the rubble around the church. One held the altar's crucifix and was carrying it away. He recalled the Children of Michael and shuddered. What he remembered about them and about what they'd said seemed too bizarre to be true. Yet all the things that had gone on recently had been just as unbelievable, fantastic and utterly scary. The woman carrying the crucifix appeared unreal, too, like a hallucination. Everything felt that way now, as if he were imagining it, as if it were all ending.

The sound of stringed instruments floated up from the

street, Fidelity's song, soft and eerily beautiful. Feeling the effects of the joint he'd smoked an hour before, he lay back on his pillow. "The final moment of pain," Fidelity rasped in a whisper. "That lovely moment of pain." As Stephen listened to the song's last chords, he felt a stirring inside himself, a sense of loss. Peter's not home, he thought; he's probably dead. Another link was gone.

With a start, he pulled himself up to the edge of the bed. A video clip of a hilly landscape in Chechnya was on the TV, the countryside ravaged. The camera zoomed in on a brown, scorched hill. Ragged children, thin and wasting, were gathered at its base, their eyes wide open and terrified.

He jumped up, searching the floor for his shoes. He could no longer hear anything coming from the street, no music or anything else. His apartment was still, the hallway outside quiet as well. His building had been that way all day. He grabbed the telephone and dialed Peter's number. There was no answer. Tottering, he found his shoes at the foot of the bed and put them on. He *had* to go to Peter's, he decided; he needed to know what had happened to him. He hadn't left his apartment since the previous morning, when he'd gone out to buy cigarettes and a sandwich. He'd felt better outside—very weird, though. He tried to place what it was that he'd felt and hesitated once more, perplexed.

At last he rushed out the door.

On the street it was at least 110 degrees, hotter than he'd ever before felt it in New York. He could hear no sirens or radios, no helicopters or planes, and he could see no cars passing by. The sun was luridly bright, and a slight breeze stirred. As it did, he could feel the effects of the pot he'd smoked lessening. It seemed as if he were just awakening, as if, at that instant, he were coming alive.

Then the heat of the sun sank into him, and he forgot what

he was doing, why he'd come out. He looked around. A small boy scurried through the doorway of a building several yards to his right. Apart from him, he could see only two people, a man and a woman, both a block away, heading east. There had been few people on the street yesterday, too. Every day since the war had broken out there had appeared to be fewer and fewer. Today it was emptier than he'd seen it since the previous Christmas, which had been a cold and stormy day. The street's being deserted now was remarkable for a late Wednesday afternoon, when many should have been returning from work. More incredible still was the contrast with the night that Moscow had been attacked, when it had been so packed. At the moment even the boys who usually hung out by the curb weren't there. He supposed a lot of people were sick, flattened by the heat or by the virulent flu going around—or maybe they were unhinged by recent events. He shivered, running a hand across his brow, then remembered that he needed to find Peter. He searched in his pockets for his cigarettes and discovered that he'd left them upstairs. He hurried toward the delicatessen on the corner.

The elderly Egyptian who owned the store was alone inside, the interior of his shop silent save for static being emitted from a radio behind him. He looked up quickly when Stephen entered, as if he were surprised to see another person. "Oh," he said, his accent thick, "it's you." He stopped, shaking his head, then sighed. "The Christians, they're going."

Stephen peered at him, incredulous. "The *Christians?*"

The old man nodded and smiled weakly. "All of them. Going. Perhaps for them it's a holiday, no?"

An announcer's voice burst through the static on the radio: "To repeat the news coming in now from Washington, the president has issued an ultimatum to Russia, demanding that it cease its hostilities immediately or face the prospect of the conflict broadening, perhaps involving NATO. No word as

yet on how the surviving members of the Russian government
have responded."

The old man nodded once more and continued to smile.
"Yes, a holiday. The Christians have gone."

Stephen found his smile disquieting. He yanked a five-dollar
bill from his pocket. "Just let me have a pack of Marlboros, okay?"

The old man's smile disappeared. He shrugged, taking the

85

bill, then found the cigarettes on the shelf above him and handed the pack to Stephen. Not waiting for his change, Stephen ran outside.

He stood in front of the store, nearly blinded by the sun, and felt fever coursing through his body. The emptiness of the street seemed to envelop him; it was as if everything had dissolved. He saw himself as he'd been a decade before, with Robert in their apartment, at a party they'd given, surrounded by friends—Sharon, Peter, and many others. He tried to bring himself back. He could feel the sun beating down on him and heard far away the sound of a radio, which was playing Fidelity's song. He listened, gazing at the street as it sparkled in the sunlight, and remembered being with Robert on a vacation they'd taken in the Southwest, riding in a car on a desert highway, the sun shimmering against the surface of the desert as Robert drove, one hand on the steering wheel, his other holding Stephen's. Stephen had felt as light as the desert appeared, completely open, the vacation having, temporarily, helped patch up their rifts. He squeezed Robert's hand and let his skin absorb the sunlight shining in through the car's window. The sun seemed to fill him with its warmth, the openness he felt allowing it to enter.

He focused on the empty street, sensing that same warmth within himself, unfamiliar for so long. He felt that the solitude had enabled this to happen and wanted to let the warmth overwhelm him, but he couldn't. Then the warmth evaporated, and he again felt only hot and completely alone. Sweat poured down his sides, and his head was pounding. He hurried north, toward Peter's, passing few people on the way.

Peter's building was an old brownstone at the corner of First Avenue and 5th Street. When Stephen arrived, the front door was open, its top hinge broken. He paused, out of breath and frightened, then pressed the buzzer, but there was no answer.

He continued waiting, his pulse throbbing. Finally, cautious, he walked through the doorway.

The building appeared empty and was silent. Afraid to make a sound, he crept up the stairs. On the third floor he found Peter's door ajar.

"Peter?" he called, his voice tremulous. "Peter?" No response. He slipped past the open door and inched his way inside.

The apartment was bright and airy, underscoring its alarming vacancy. "Peter?" he called one last time, but he knew this was useless. The space was small, a studio, and Peter would have heard him by now.

He stared at the familiar room, detecting just a hint of cologne in the air, a lovely scent he'd never before encountered. Peter's bed was to the left of him, against a white wall, unmade. He walked to it and sat down. There was a magazine lying by the pillow, opened to the personals ads. He picked it up and looked at its cover. Stunned, he saw that it was *Dewy Boys*.

He gripped the magazine tightly, then very slowly flipped through it to the pictures of Dano. He became absorbed by them and by the heat in the air, sensing inside himself the same warmth that he'd experienced outside. He felt in some way connected to the air around him and glanced up at the empty apartment, at that moment certain—he had no idea why—that Peter was gone for good.

He veered his head toward a fireplace to his left. Peter liked to keep a fire burning on wintry nights. He recalled standing there with Robert and Peter on a frigid evening in January, during one of his and Robert's frequent visits. They had known Peter so well—his long, rather solemn face, his thin brown hair, his hospitality and brittle humor—and used to call him their "marriage counselor." They'd come here to get away from themselves and be distracted.

That night they'd all talked about a new band whose show they'd seen. "It's a wig, you know," Peter remarked dryly, speaking about the drummer's wavy hair. He giggled. "I mean, come on, nothing's *that* perfect." Stephen was high and found this hilarious. Overcome by laughter, he leaned against Robert, holding onto his arm. It felt uncommonly thin, and his laughter stopped. He drew his hand away and tried to forget what he'd just observed. But within six months, Robert's deterioration had become so obvious, to him and to everyone else, that he could no longer disregard anything.

He quickly looked down at the magazine in his hands, at Dano's bronzed skin, then turned back to where it had been opened, to the personals. An ad was there, one that he'd never before noticed. It was in the midst of the usual displays of shirtless, chiselled men, advertisements for phone-sex numbers, masseurs, and escort services. "The Boy of Your Dreams," it read in large, bold type. "From the World's Most Trustworthy Agency." At the bottom was a telephone number. The ad was similar to the others, save for the photograph it used, a misty head shot, not of a shirtless man, but of a beautiful, smiling, and, it seemed, ethereal boy, one who, Stephen felt, looked a lot like Dano—or like Robert when he'd been young.

Trembling, he wondered if this really was the same issue he owned. Everything else was the same: the pictures of Dano, the other photo spreads of nude, Czechoslovakian youths. He reached into his shirt pocket, grabbed his pack of cigarettes, and lit one, moving his eyes to the agency's phone number. He couldn't understand why Peter had left this magazine out, opened to this page. He became more conscious of the room's heat and its emptiness, then envisioned Robert, longing for him. In a precipitous motion, he leaped up, the magazine in his hand, and rushed from the apartment.

A cab was passing Peter's building when Stephen ran out, the only car on the street. He hailed it. As the cab pulled over for him, he remembered that he had just a few dollars left. He didn't care. Only two more unemployment checks were due

him before his benefits were depleted, but this, too, seemed
unimportant. He climbed into the cab, glancing out its window. A plastic bag full of cans had been ripped open, and most
of its contents had spilled onto the sidewalk. Everything
around him appeared desolate, and he recalled the Children
of Michael. Shit, he thought, the world *is* ending.

The driver, a middle-aged black man with dreadlocks, took
off without waiting for Stephen to give him directions. Though

Stephen couldn't understand why, he felt as if this man knew where he wanted to go. He spoke to him anyway: "Houston and Ridge, southwest corner." The driver looked back at him and grinned. The cab sped through the empty streets.

Once home, Stephen found his own copy of *Dewy Boys* and compared it to the one he'd brought from Peter's. The ad was there, the boy in the photograph looking even more like Robert as Stephen studied him again. He sensed himself being drawn into the photo, to the boy. He wanted to sleep, but was convinced that he wouldn't be able to, and considered getting high, then remembered that he'd smoked his last joint and that he had no alcohol left. He switched on the TV and watched a fire raging through a hillside village, out of control. In the background he heard an announcer's voice: "It's clear that the Russians have ignored the president's ultimatum. Indeed, they appear to be thumbing their noses at him. The question at the moment is how the president will respond to this latest outrage." Stephen's heart was pounding. He turned down the TV's sound, swerved toward the telephone, grabbed the receiver, and dialed Sharon.

When she answered, she sounded as frightened as he was. "Oh, Stephen," she cried, "I can't talk. Something's happened."

"*What*? What's that?"

"It's my dad. He...I mean, I think..." She paused to catch her breath. Then, desperate: "And...and my mom. She's sick now, too."

Stephen clutched the receiver and glanced down at the two magazines, side by side on his bed, at the advertisement.

"Let me go, okay?" Sharon was frantic. "*Please.* Mom's calling me." She hung up.

Stephen held onto the receiver, reeling. His eyes returned to the ad. Seeing the boy soothed him. He found him so much like Robert, his black hair and his smile practically the same, like Dano, too, Dano in that forest, in the picture he loved.

He wished he were in those woods, with Robert—or maybe alone, like when he was a child. He glanced at the agency's phone number, then at the telephone. Behind it, against the wall, he could see the television set, the fire in the village still on its screen. He focused on the telephone again, then dialed.

A man picked up. "Yes?"

His voice startled Stephen: It was deep and even, and sounded like his father's. He almost hung up.

"You're calling about our ad, aren't you?"

Despite the similarity that Stephen had detected, the man's tone was soft, and he seemed kind—kind and very wise. Stephen couldn't imagine his father being like that, though he'd often wished he were. He opened his mouth. "Ye…yeah." Once he'd spoken, he was shocked that he'd managed to say anything.

The man chuckled. "You like the boy, don't you? The one in our ad? That's who you want, isn't it?"

Stephen tightened his hold on the receiver.

"Of course you do. Everyone does. We all love Michael."

Stephen couldn't believe what the man had just said. He sucked in his breath, gazing at the boy in the advertisement, then up at the television screen. Flames were devouring a court building on the village's square.

"I can send him over to you now if you'd like. We can talk about payment later."

Stephen watched as the building collapsed. "Yes," he heard himself say. "I want to see him." His voice sounded remote to him, as if not his own.

"Good." As the man spoke, Stephen imagined him smiling. "Good, good. He'll be there in an hour."

Stephen heard a click, and the man was gone. He felt excited, strangely enthralled, but then, in a flash, realized he'd never given the man his address. He dialed the agency's number again. It was busy. A news anchor appeared on the television screen, his face grimly determined. Stephen turned up the sound.

"Reports of a nuclear explosion in the vicinity of Jerusalem have been neither confirmed nor denied," the anchor was saying. "Despite this uncertainty, a terrorist group, LATA, has already claimed responsibility. According to sources in the

Pentagon, if the attack did occur, there is a real danger that, through happenstance, the Russian conflict could spread to the Middle East."

Stephen switched off the TV. He hesitated, unsure what he could do, then abruptly grabbed the telephone receiver and tried the agency once more. He reached a recording: "The number you dialed is no longer in service. No further details are available. Please consult your directory." He threw the receiver aside and lay down, sweating and feverish.

I'm dreaming, he told himself, caught up, it seemed, by the heat in the air; I'm dreaming or dead. He thought then about the man at the agency, remembered how he'd mentioned the boy, Michael, and felt the way he had as a child, when he was very young and his parents still seemed good, far off in their own world, yet comforting, like that man. He recalled Christmas as it had been when he was six years old, a Christmas he had thought about many times during those last years with Robert, when he'd needed so much. For that Christmas he'd wanted a puppy more than anything, and his mother had told him that he had to be very good in order to get one, so he had been, as good as gold for weeks.

On Christmas morning, after breakfast, Ethel took him to his parents in the living room, where they kept the Christmas tree. There, among dozens of glittering wrapped packages, was a little cocker spaniel, a huge green ribbon around his tiny brown neck. Stephen was ecstatic. But when he tried to play with his new pet, the puppy seemed lethargic and didn't respond.

He was worse the next day, totally listless and obviously ill. Stephen's mother had a servant take him to the vet. That night at dinner she told Stephen that his puppy had been put to sleep.

"I know it's hard for you," she said slowly, her voice uncharacteristically gentle, "but these things happen." For that moment she looked empathic, her eyes motherly, the way he'd seen them only a few times. She patted his hand. Then, as if

93

embarrassed by any feelings she might have revealed, she drew away, raising a forkful of peas to her red lips. "It probably wasn't such a good idea for us to get him in the first place," she went on, more reserved. "You would have forgotten about him in a day or two anyway. And puppies make such messes."

Stephen started crying, as distraught by his mother's withdrawal as he was by his puppy's death. His father rapped his arm, using a heavy gold ring he wore. "Be a man!" he exclaimed. Stephen tried very hard to obey and was finally able to stop. He knew after this not to expect much.

Music drifted in through an open window, pulling him back: "Oh, that moment of pain. Give me that moment of pain." Drenched in sweat, he sat up, overwhelmed by a need that he couldn't understand. The song sounded unbearably sad. "Robert?" he asked, aloud but softly. Then, more faintly: "Michael?"

The need he felt remained as the music faded, and he lay down again.

2

He sensed the warmth and a light directly above him, a light he'd seen before, in a dream, perhaps, or maybe somewhere else. He felt a breeze, just a slight one, but it was enough to cut through the room's heat and make the temperature tolerable, even pleasant. He wasn't certain, but he suspected that his fever had lifted.

Then he saw a boy standing by the wall several feet from his bed, smiling down at him, beautifully ethereal, so lovely that he seemed almost blank, like a screen. He felt himself smiling back. He knew this had to be Michael.

"Hey," Michael said brightly, greeting him. "You've been asleep."

95

Stephen gazed at his thick black hair, then at his tawny skin and his blue T-shirt and jeans. His body appeared relaxed, supple like an adolescent's, and, just as Stephen had observed in the magazine's photograph, he did look very much like Dano and, even more distinctly, like Robert. Yet he seemed so much more concrete than any photograph could be, than any vision Stephen may have had, so *present*. Stephen felt as if he'd never before seen anyone so completely real.

"Your door was open," Michael went on, his voice mellifluous, "so I let myself in. I hope you don't mind."

"No." Stephen couldn't take his eyes off him. All other considerations save Michael's presence vanished. "I…I think I've been waiting for you."

"Right." Michael grinned. "It's been busy lately."

Stephen contemplated his age and decided he looked at most eighteen. He sensed the breeze and at that moment felt eighteen himself. He wanted to touch Michael's arm, his skin, for it appeared incredibly smooth, but he felt as if he couldn't breathe and did nothing.

Michael broke the silence. Still smiling, he said, "Well, what do you want us to do? You know, do you want to talk? Do you want me to undress?" He lowered his right hand to the bottom of his T-shirt, looking as if he were about to lift the shirt over his head.

Stephen drew back. He'd caught a distinctly musical quality in Michael's voice, which, when taken with the breeze in the room, reminded him of Ethel and Robert. Moving his eyes toward the bedroom window, he saw that it was pitch-black outside, apparently much later than he'd thought. He returned to Michael. "What…what was that?" he asked, faltering.

Michael's smile disappeared, and his expression became one of a powerfully benevolent concern. He waited for an instant, then gently said, "You *did* want me to come, didn't you? I mean, they told me you called."

Stephen stared at Michael's eyes, which were large and brown, recalling how he and Robert used to lie in bed, entwined, just before making love. It seemed as if Robert's eyes at those times had been as Michael's were now, filled with an openness that promised so much.

Both hands now at the bottom of his T-shirt, Michael moved closer to the bed, then spoke faintly: "What would you like?"

Stephen wanted Michael next to him, wanted this desperately. "*Please*," he said.

Michael gazed back at him. "Yes?"

"Please undress." The urgency that Stephen heard in his own voice was staggering.

Michael smiled once more. "That's what you want?" His tone was very kind. "That's what you *really* want?" He raised his T-shirt, revealing a firm, hairless belly, then slowly pulled the shirt over his head and removed it. He stood still.

Stephen studied his smooth chest, thinking about the times he and Robert had made love on hot summer nights, their chests pressed together, their skin moist with sweat as they embraced. He felt a pang inside himself and, just slightly, lifted an arm, beckoning Michael to come to him.

Michael lowered a hand to his jeans, unzipped them, and let them drop. Naked, he inched forward.

Stephen watched him approach, awed by his glowing skin; his taut, perfectly formed body; his thickly veined penis and lush, black pubic hair.

Michael sat on the bed next to Stephen, leaning toward him. "Do you want us to make love?" he whispered.

Stephen wanted to kiss Michael, take him in his arms, but was afraid to let himself. He was overcome by Michael's beauty, his manner, his calm. It made him think of the past, of what he'd missed. He was shaking and felt tears well up in his eyes.

"Hey." Michael touched Stephen's arm. "Hey, what's the matter?"

The tears streamed down Stephen's face, and he started to cry, his body racked by his sobs.

Michael threw his arms around Stephen, pulling his head to his chest. "Come on, what's going on? It's going to be all right." He kissed his cheek. "Really. Everything's going to be fine."

Stephen pressed his face against Michael, thinking that he smelled sweeter than anyone he'd ever met. He wanted to believe what he'd said and, just for a second, let his lips brush against his chest. Then, through the remains of his tears, he saw the TV. It was off, but he knew what he'd see there if it were on. He pushed himself away from Michael, shaking again.

Michael pulled him back and held onto him. "Don't. *Please.* Stay with me."

Stephen wanted to relax and embrace Michael, yet felt unable to. He started to cry once more, softly this time. "It's too late. It's all over."

"What is?" Michael stroked Stephen's back.

"Everything, fucking everything." Pulling away, Stephen glanced toward the TV, then back at Michael. "The world's exploding!"

Michael produced a dim smile. He hesitated briefly, then said, "But maybe this is just the beginning. I mean, things are changing, and that's scary. Perhaps, though...Well, maybe it'll all get much better."

Stephen heard a lilt in Michael's voice, and it drew him in. For that moment he believed what he'd said. Then he thought of what was going on, of his miserable life. "That'll never happen!" He laughed bitterly. "What's the point of even thinking about it?"

Michael peered at him. His smile became wider and kinder. Stephen peered back, hearing the words he'd read days earlier, coming from he knew not where: "And at that time shall Michael stand up, the great prince which standeth for the children of the people." His eyes darted down to Michael's tanned chest and to his groin. He shivered yet felt wonderfully warm. He wanted to lie down and pull Michael with him, to accept the warmth.

"A lot of things happened, didn't they?" Michael asked. "You know, when you were young. That's why this is all so hard for you, isn't it?"

"*What?*" Stephen felt the muscles in his back tighten. "What're you talking about? How...?"

"Come on." Michael grinned. "You know who I am. You asked for me."

Stephen gazed into Michael's eyes, sensing just then that he knew everything, all about Robert, his parents, what he'd suffered. Charlene and the others had known much of this, too. They'd told him about Michael. They'd been right.

Michael took hold of Stephen's right hand. "You do know what's going on, don't you?"

"I…" Stephen leaned toward Michael, then sank onto his chest.

"It's important for you to try and accept everything, accept the past and move forward to God."

Stephen's pulse was throbbing. He squeezed his eyes shut, taking in Michael's words and the lovely scent of his skin.

"When you've started to do that," Michael went on, "things will clear up, and you'll understand."

Stephen opened his eyes. Michael was smiling down on him sweetly. "Understand?"

Michael gazed at him even more kindly. "What's about to happen to you."

Stephen was certain that he knew what Michael was talking about, but he still felt compelled to speak: "And…and what's that?"

Michael moved one of his hands up Stephen's side, caressing him. "Don't worry," he said soothingly. "There's so much you're going to learn. It'll all come to you."

Stephen kept his eyes fixed on Michael's face, at the same time picturing his mother and father at their dinner table, alone and very old. He saw himself in those woods, and he was old now, too. He wanted to join his parents and forgive them. Then the woods became immersed in a vivid light. He refocused on Michael, and the things that had preyed on him no longer seemed to matter. Everything—his childhood, Robert's death, his loneliness, the war, even his desperation at Muffin's and the desolation of the street today—appeared to be swirling into Michael's eyes and dissolving.

Michael spoke calmly and evenly: "You're learning now."

Stephen continued staring at him. His face was amazingly placid, maddeningly so, his chest smooth and tan, his groin inviting. Stephen felt frustrated—by what he'd never had, all he'd lost, what he wanted but was afraid to take. I'm just with a whore, he told himself; that's all Michael is. He studied Michael's glistening chest. The light it appeared to project provided an astonishing contrast to the blackness that was visible through the window. More frustrated, he wanted to do something, *anything*. He lifted a hand and grazed Michael's chest with it, then pulled back. "I want to fuck you," he mumbled.

Appearing both quizzical and solicitous, Michael gazed at him. "Isn't there something else you'd like?"

"What do you…?" Stephen wavered, confused, and the frustration he'd felt became anger. He hesitated for a few seconds longer, his eyes locked on Michael's, sensing his tranquility. Quivering, in an abrupt movement, he threw himself against him, pushing him down onto the bed and falling on top of him, pressing himself against his nude body. He could feel Michael beneath him, uncommonly still and warm. He wanted to take off his own clothes but, gasping, wasn't sure that he could. All of his muscles grew rigid, and he stopped moving.

"Relax." Michael ran a hand across Stephen's shoulders. "You don't have to do anything. Just come to me."

Stephen sank into Michael's skin. It was as if he were becoming a part of him, part of Robert, part of everyone who'd ever lived, part of the world.

"This is just the beginning," Michael told him.

He was one with Michael, he knew this. All else had disappeared, and he clung to him. Hours seemed to pass. They were drifting through a beautiful void.

Then, in this space, he heard Michael's voice, very close to him: "I'm sorry, but it's time for me to leave. There're things I have to do."

Stephen felt himself returning. He sat up, pulling away from Michael. "You...you're leaving?"

Michael smiled, stroking Stephen's thigh. "Not for long. It's just that I have clients who need to see me, clients in L.A."

Stephen didn't say anything. Instead he started to tremble, rocking back and forth.

With great emotion, Michael threw his arms around him. "Look, I'll be back. Very, very soon. Believe me, I will. Everything'll get better."

Stephen felt as if Michael's voice were rippling through him, as if he were going to some earlier time, to his childhood or, perhaps, to Robert, to before what they'd had grew sullied. He stopped rocking and fell against Michael.

"You understand?" Michael kneaded his back. "You can trust us. You do know that, don't you?"

Stephen looked up at Michael. Holding onto him, he moved his lips to his mouth.

Michael kissed him—lovingly, for a very long time. At last he drew away. "Just remember," he said, "we'll be with you." He embraced Stephen once more, tightly against his chest. Then he faded and was gone.

3

Suddenly alone, Stephen looked around. It seemed as if Michael had never been here. Yet nothing appeared the same. It was light outside, sunny and again very hot. The blackness had vanished. And the apartment itself felt different; everything was somehow more focused and sharper. It seemed as if days had passed, even weeks.

Unsteady, he leaned forward and switched on the TV. The news anchor he'd seen earlier was on. "This just in from

Washington," he was saying, his voice tense. "Sources at the White House have informed us that the president has initiated a tactical nuclear strike against Libya in retaliation for its role in yesterday's devastation of Israel. There's been no word from the president as yet, but a press conference is scheduled imminently."

His pulse racing, Stephen muted the TV and glanced toward the window. The blackness had returned; it appeared to be nighttime again. He leaned toward the bedside table and grasped his cigarettes. The pack was empty. He stared out the window, trying to understand what was happening. Very slowly he sensed himself becoming part of the blackness. This was not unpleasant. In some way it seemed to him that he was moving closer to Michael, to the peace that he'd felt in his presence. As he became more absorbed in this feeling, it again grew light outside.

He recoiled, stunned, then grabbed the telephone receiver and dialed Sharon's number, needing to hear her voice. Her phone rang. It rang and rang and rang, but there was no answer. He tried once more. There was still no answer. His eyes darted toward the window. The blackness had come back.

Shaking, he turned up the TV's sound. Another anchor was speaking, one he'd never before seen, a large, graying woman dressed in a dark blue business suit. She looked haggard and pale, perhaps ill.

"The consensus here is that the president's actions have been a complete success," she intoned, making an effort to be brisk, yet clearly enfeebled. "Libya has been crushed, her forces neutralized. Now, however, we must contend with the reaction of Russia, Libya's firm ally, which, though much weakened by its recent wars, still has a huge arsenal of nuclear weapons left over from its days as the center of the Soviet Union. It's apparent in the president's bearing that he's extremely concerned by the silence coming from those quarters."

Stephen froze. It all seemed to be happening so quickly. He veered toward the bedside table and clutched his cigarettes. He discovered once again that he had none left. He darted up from the bed, glancing toward the window. The sky was now shifting rapidly between blackness and light. He stood still, nearly overcome by terror and the heat. The sky appeared to settle into daylight, and he hesitated, dripping with sweat, not certain what to do. Then he rushed outside.

There was no one on the street, no pedestrians or cars, and it was totally silent, the humidity suffocating. The bright light and complete emptiness of his surroundings seemed to pierce him, until he felt as if they had become part of him. For a moment he saw nothing but brightness. Then he became aware of the sky, which appeared remarkably, startlingly blue. It seemed to reflect the silence and emptiness around him. He tried to run toward the Egyptian's store, but he couldn't, weak, sick, and frightened as he felt. Unendurably hot, wheezing, he staggered along as quickly as he could, not very quickly at all.

The store was closed, its metal gate down. He'd never before seen it shut; day or night, someone in the Egyptian owner's family always seemed to be there. He looked to his left, then across the street to his right. Every other shop he saw—the hardware store, the Chinese restaurant, the dry cleaner, and the laundromat—was shut as well.

He sank toward the ground and cringed by the store, then, shivering from his fever, thought for a moment that he was dispersing, his body merging with the heat, becoming one with the air. The desolation around him appeared harshly bright, evanescent, too, as if it could vanish at any second. This frightened him and made him think of his night at Muffin's, about Davey and the others, how threatening everything had felt. He stared at the sparkling pavement, and it seemed like he was floating. He recalled himself at six, going to Ethel's church, walking with her down a street in his hometown, holding her hand. He had felt completely secure, safe and at peace, and he wanted to feel that way now. The pavement continued to sparkle, and he seemed to continue to float, and he realized that, in fact, he was starting to feel like that.

I'm going to Robert, he told himself, sure that he was wafting higher; it'll be just like the old days. But would it? Couldn't all that they'd experienced, all they'd felt—couldn't those feelings have come about merely because they'd been young? *This* could be totally different.

He gazed at the sky; it was growing black again. He heard the sound of an airplane shattering the silence and saw it flying low over Queens, descending toward Kennedy Airport. The sky became inky, the lights of the plane more prominent. Then, with a rush of great noise, the plane exploded and burst into flames. It began to fall.

Shaken to his depths, he stared at the flames raining down in the distance, against the black, starless sky, above the dark buildings around him. The brightness of the flames colored everything with a dazzling orange-red glow. He felt hypnotized by what he saw and didn't move. But then his heart leapt, pounding powerfully. It seemed to him that he was falling with the flames, returning to the earth, and he bolted upward. He hurried home as quickly as he was able to.

As soon as he got there, he picked up the phone. It was dead. He tossed the receiver aside and turned on the TV. He could see nothing but static. Beneath this, he heard a man exclaiming, "The disaster around Kennedy is unparalleled!" The voice faded, and he gazed at the television screen. A face appeared, partially obscured by the static, that of the graying, haggard woman in the blue business suit. "Something seems to have happened in California!" she cried, in shock. "We've lost all contact with our West Coast affiliates. Rumors are circulating that there has been a powerful earthquake in the vicinity of Los Angeles, but these haven't been confirmed. Even so, it's...it's as if everything in the area is gone!"

Michael! Stephen thought. Terrified, he rolled off of the bed and fell to his knees, glancing back at the television screen, seeing through the static dim images of a fire racing across a cityscape, in California or in Queens, maybe somewhere else, he didn't know. He pressed his face against the bedsheets, want-

ing to pray, then looked up, out the window. The sky was blue, then black. He swerved his eyes toward the TV and saw the static on the screen clearing into an advertisement he knew well, one showing two blond boys tap-dancing in synch while holding large radios. This gave way to the station's yellow logo and to the words, "Countdown to War."

He stared out the window. The blackness remained.

PART III
RAPTURE

In the hour before Russia's attack, Stephen thought of the time he'd gone to church with Ethel, back when he was six. He lay on his bed, feverish and weak, and his memories surged up like dreams, a part of the stifling air, coming, it seemed, on a breeze that wasn't there.

He remembered that Sunday, just before going to church, sitting on Ethel's lap and sobbing, distressed by his puppy's death, by what his mother had done. Ethel had patted his head and pulled him closer. "Trust God," she whispered. "It'll all come out right." After she spoke, so softly, he pushed his face against her chest, into her warmth, smelling her heavy, sweet perfume. He thought that he could feel a glow coming from her depths, which seemed to draw him even closer to her. He stopped crying but remained as he was, pressed against her, sucking his thumb, almost forgetting about what had occurred, at peace.

This feeling stayed with him throughout the morning. He and Ethel walked to her church, and as they did, he thought it a special treat to be going with her; she'd never before taken him there. His parents didn't know she was doing this; they were with friends. Enjoying the adventure, he held onto Ethel's hand, basking in her love.

When they arrived, they sat on one of the church's hard pews. Everything seemed magical: the old wooden church, packed with black parishioners; the short, white-haired preacher at the pulpit; the light shining dimly through stained-glass windows; the over-heated air.

"Hallelujah!" the preacher called out, in a resounding voice that belied his size.

Stephen felt absorbed by his deep, even tone. Studying the parishioners' rapt faces, he clutched Ethel's hand more tight-

ly, then felt a pleasant warmth run up his spine. He smiled. "Hallelujah," he whispered.

"Fear God," the preacher continued, reading from the Bible, his voice quivering with passion. "Give glory to Him, for the hour of His judgment is come."

"Praise God!" Ethel answered fervently.

Stephen was moved, stirred by the fact that this woman who loved him had spoken so devoutly. "Praise God," he said, his voice still a whisper but his words more distinct.

The preacher read of the coming Apocalypse and of the Judgment of God: "And I saw the dead, small and great, stand before God...The sea gave up the dead which were in it, and death and hell gave up the dead which were in them; and they were judged every man according to their works."

Stephen knew what he was talking about; Ethel had told him about Judgment Day many times. God and Jesus were going to return to Earth. There'd be fire and disease and storms. A trumpet would blast, and God's horsemen would gallop across the sky, preparing the way. Then God would appear, Jesus at His side, and behind them, everyone who'd ever lived. Love would be everywhere.

"Yes, Jesus!" people cried. "Hallelujah!"

"Praise the Lord!" Perspiring, the preacher closed his eyes.

Stephen listened to him and to the prayers of the congregation, sensing joy amid the light in the air. He felt like he could fly, like nothing outside mattered, and clung to Ethel's hand. "Hallelujah!" he heard himself say, loudly and happily.

The couple sitting in the pew in front of Ethel, a fat woman and a very thin man wearing a bow tie, looked back and smiled kindly at him.

"Oh, child," Ethel murmured. She leaned over and hugged Stephen.

Embarrassed by the couple's attention, Stephen sank into Ethel's dress.

"Jesus will be with us again!" the preacher shouted.

Stephen saw parishioners behind Ethel raising their hands and rejoicing. Caught up in the warmth of Ethel's embrace and by the love that he had for her, he felt his embarrassment fade. The congregation started singing a gospel tune, and the joy he was experiencing washed over him. He was convinced that despite what his mother had done or whatever might happen, he'd be fine. Ethel was with him; God was with her.

Inert on his bed, Stephen remembered this, wanting his memories to comfort him. But his life—the world— appeared to be reeling toward the blackness outside. It seemed like Michael had been the last bit of hope and that only the past remained—though somehow, distantly, the hope that Michael had brought with him lingered.

He stared at the static on the television screen, hearing muffled voices beneath it; he couldn't make out the words. He looked toward the window, at the blackness, which seemed to have been there for hours, perhaps for days. It was so dark that he could see nothing at all. He heard a man's strained, hoarse voice coming from the TV: "All we can do is pray." He kept his eyes on the window, longing for Michael, for Robert, to be connected to that past, the joy he'd felt in church so long ago. He wiped his brow. The room was spinning. "Hallelujah," he whispered numbly.

Suddenly, outside, beneath the blackness, in what could have been the sky, he saw a tiny golden light, so faint it was almost imperceptible. The room stopped spinning, and the light grew stronger, until it was so bright that it glared. He felt drawn to it, as if he could float in its direction.

His buzzer rang, and the light disappeared.

All of his muscles tensed. The blackness outside returned, and he sensed it entering him. He began shaking. He wanted to leap through the window, float in the sky.

There was a rap at his door. He jumped up and spun around.

Michael stood by the bedroom's doorway, naked. "See," he said to Stephen, "I wasn't long, was I?"

Michael's skin looked soft, so smooth and familiar. He appeared just as he had earlier, achingly desirable. Yet his very essence seemed to be changing—Stephen couldn't see precisely how—shifting subtly, turning into something Stephen had lost a long time before. A feeling of calm came over him, then joy.

"Come here." Michael raised his arms toward Stephen. "Let's go together."

A man's voice boomed out from the television set: "We can't reach Washington! Something's going on!"

Stephen hurried to Michael and threw his arms around him, grasping his back, pushing himself against his skin. He kissed and caressed him, felt his touch. He thought that he could feel the change in him that he'd noticed, elusive yet definitely there. The golden light he'd seen outside was in the room, incredibly bright and lovely.

He looked up. It was now Robert he was holding, the younger Robert, the Robert he'd fallen in love with, naked as Michael had been. He felt dazzled. It was as if he were holding an unspoiled part of themselves.

"Hello," Robert said, smiling. He hugged Stephen tightly and kissed his lips.

Stephen took in Robert's sweet smell, the wonderful warmth of the room, of his embrace, his lips. He thought of the two of them years earlier, entwined in bed.

"I'm here," Robert whispered. "I'm back."

Stephen sensed himself floating with Robert, then the two of them alighting on the bed. The room started to dissolve.

Robert unfastened Stephen's pants. Stephen clung to him, trembling. The golden light was all around them. Robert took hold of Stephen's penis. Erect, Stephen pulled himself closer.

The television announcer could be heard again, this time crying, "We have to ask that you stay inside!"

Stephen felt Robert's lips on his skin, moving down his groin. He thought of what he'd missed, how his parents had hurt him. He'd lost something so simple, a feeling like he'd had that day in church. He wanted love.

Robert took Stephen's penis in his mouth, and Stephen was overcome by light. He let the light's warmth sink into him. He felt Robert's lips on his shaft.

"It's happening!" the announcer screamed, in both terror and awe. "Jesus, yes, it's happening!"

There was silence, then a roar, and the light came into him. He felt himself slipping away—his weight, his skin, his pain, his life. He saw the walls of the apartment, just dimly, an ephemeral, transparent presence. Clouds drifted behind them in a sky that was perfectly blue. There were shapes in the sky, an infinite number of them, all so fluid that he couldn't tell what they were.

Robert grasped Stephen's penis. Stephen pushed it inside him, still gazing at the sky, which appeared impossibly close, as if just beyond the bed, just outside the vanishing walls. He thought that he could see four nude men on white horses galloping across it, behind them an infinitude of people.

Robert moaned, and Stephen pushed further into him. In the sky, among the throng, he saw Michael, smiling at him; Ethel, his cat Rose by her feet; Sharon and Peter; Timothy, Ruth, and Charlene; the Egyptian shopkeeper; the dreadlocked boy from the fire; many, many more. All were only vaguely defined and yet, he felt, undeniably present. He pulled his penis out of Robert, then pushed it inside him once more and ejaculated.

"Yes!" Robert cried. He and Stephen rose into the air.

Holding tightly to Robert, Stephen saw beside them in the sky all of the friends he'd ever had, then, on the ground, those woods he'd loved as a child and the pond there, in a clearing bright with sunshine, filled with warmth. Beyond the woods, where his parents' house had been, were an empty lot and an endless green field. He floated toward them, shouting happily, "Hallelujah!"

"Amen," Robert said, and they descended.

Also from Akashic Books:

Massage by Henry Flesh
1999 Lamba Literary Award Winner
384 pages, trade paperback
ISBN: 1-888451-06-8
Price: $15.95
"Funny, tightly plotted, and just two shades darker than burnt coffee. Henry Flesh has crafted a fine and disturbing novel." —David Sedaris, author of *Naked*

The Big Mango by Norman Kelley
270 pages, trade paperback
ISBN: 1-888451-10-6
Price: $14.95
She's back. Nina Halligan, Private Investigator.
Critical praise for Kelly's first novel, *Black Heat*: "The plot involves an ass-kicking black female private investigator, Nina Halligan, who…crosses many strata of late-90s black society: militantly Afrocentric nationalists, middle-class buppies who've moved to Connecticut, a gutsy streetwalker, some gangstas…and a preacher with his nose so far up the Man's ass he's actually developed a scheme to franchise churches in black neighborhoods nationwide, a kind of Big Mac Baptist Church, Inc.…*Black Heat* reads like a 'philosophical novel'…" —*New York Press*

Kamikaze Lust by Lauren Sanders
280 pages, trade paperback
ISBN: 1-888451-08-4
Price: $14.95
"*Kamikaze Lust* puts a snappy spin on a traditional theme—young woman in search of herself—and stands it on its head. In a crackling, rapid-fire voice studded with deadpan one-liners and evocative descriptions, Rachel Silver takes us to such far-flung places as a pompous charity benefit, the set of an "art porn" movie, her best friend's body, Las Vegas casinos, and the psyche of her own porn-star alter ego, Silver Ray, all knit together by the unspoken question: Who am I, anyway? And as Rachel tells it, asking the question is more fun than knowing for sure could ever be."
—Kate Christensen, author of *In the Drink*

Manhattan Loverboy by Arthur Nersesian
195 pages, trade paperback
ISBN: 1-888451-09-2
Price: $13.95
"Nersesian's newest novel is a paranoid fantasy and fantastic comedy in the service of social realism, using methods of L. Frank Baum's *Wizard of Oz* or Kafka's *The Trial* to update the picaresque urban chronicles of Augie March, with a far darker edge…"
—*Downtown Magazine*

The Fuck-Up by Arthur Nersesian
274 pages, trade paperback
ISBN: 1-888451-03-3
Price: $13.00
(*Out of print. Available only through direct mail order.*)
"The charm and grit of Nersesian's voice is immediately enveloping, as the down-and-out but oddly up narrator of his terrific novel, *The Fuck-Up*, slinks through Alphabet City and guttural utterances of love." —*The Village Voice*

Once There Was a Village by Yuri Kapralov
163 pages, trade paperback
ISBN: 1-888451-05-X
Price: $12.00
"This was the era which saw the 'invasion' of hippies and junkies and swarms of runaway boys and girls who became prey to pimps, tactical police and East Village violence...In this personal memoir of his experiences, Kapralov relives the squalor and hazards of community life along Seventh Street between Avenues B and C. The street riots of 1966, the break-up of his own stormy marriage, poignant or amusing but always memorably etched stories of the Slavs, Russians, Puerto Ricans, blacks and artists young and old who were his neighbors, his own breakdown—all of it makes a 'shtetl' experience that conjures up something of Gorki and Chagall."
—*Publisher's Weekly*

These books are available at local bookstores. They can also be purchased with a credit card online through www.akashicbooks.com. To order by mail or to order out-of-print titles, send a check or money order to:
Akashic Books
PO Box 1456
New York, NY 10009
www.akashicbooks.com
(Prices include shipping. Outside the U.S., add $3 to each book ordered.)

Henry Flesh dropped out of Yale in the sixties and spent many of the ensuing years abroad, in London, Crete, and Morocco. His first novel, *Massage*, won the 1999 Lambda Literary Award for Best Title from a Small Press. He currently lives in New York City and works as an editor for *People* magazine.

Illustrator John H. Greer grew up in southern Virginia and studied art at Virginia Commonwealth University and Hunter College. He belonged to a right-wing Christian cult for five years, but has since become enlightened and is now an artist living in Manhattan's Lower East Side.